LOVECRAFT'S PILLOW

AND OTHER WEIRD TALES

LOVECRAFT'S PILLOW

AND OTHER WEIRD TALES

K. SCOTT FORMAN

FEAR KNOCKS PRESS

Fear Knocks Press
2044 West 1890 South
Woods Cross, Utah 84087

Library of Congress Cataloging-in-Publication Data
ISBN-13: 978-1-7322446-0-3
ISBN-10: 1-73224460-X
LCCN: 2018904608

First printing: April 2018

10 9 8 7 6 5 4 3 2 1

Printed in the United States of America
First Electronic Edition: April 2018

ISBN-13: 978-1-7322446-1-0
ISBN-10: 1-7322446-1-8

Cover Design: SelfPubBookCovers.com/Daniela

Formatting: www.FireDrakeDesigns.com

Visit www.fearknocks.com for blog, current news, and other mojo.

For Seymour,
Celeste,
Ali & Daniel

CONTENTS

FOREWORD

Where would I be without Mary Shelley, Bram Stoker, and Robert Louis Stevenson? I love the Gothic; love everything about it, especially the darkness, and I think what brought me to these three would have been Edgar Allan Poe and the Bible, especially the Old Testament. Something about evil and the dark have always fascinated me. The stories of the Sons of God and daughters of men procreating and creating a race of giants, or Cain and Abel complete with Lucifer: can it really get any better for horror? As a child, I read the Bible and Poe's short stories. *The Black Cat, The Cask of Amontillado*, and all the rest set me on a path to find the great writers of Gothic horror and more.

Several of the stories in this collection found their roots in the gloom and doom of those early fashioners of terror and the macabre. I was fortunate in finding homes for them in trade publications, anthologies, and the like, but others, included in this volume, are just now seeing the light of day.

The impetus that starts most of my writing can be found in reading, and in reading widely. H. P. Lovecraft, Shirley Jackson, Robert R. McCammon, Joe R. Landsdale, and even Stephen King, along with Shelley, Stoker, Stevenson, and Poe have found space in my library. Shakespeare, William Blake and Samuel Taylor Coleridge, and even Sylvia Plath and Anne Sexton are as familiar as J. K. Rowling, and J. R. R. Tolkien. Gabriel Garcia Marquez and Isabel Allende share space with Elizabeth Kostova and Jim Butcher, and even Barbara Louise Mertz

(Elizabeth Peters) makes a guest appearance. Reading opens up vistas and allows me to live other lives. Joyce Carol Oates said, *Reading is the sole means by which we slip, involuntarily, often helplessly, into another's skin, another's voice, another's soul.* I would agree.

Lastly, I must credit Stephen King in his foreword to Michel Houelle-becq's *H.P. Lovecraft: Against the World, Against Life* as the seed for this collection. I hope you, Gentle Reader, enjoy reading the stories as much as I enjoyed writing them. They are *Weird Tales*.

13 April 2018 (Friday)

ACKNOWLEDGMENTS

"Expendable," by K. Scott Forman: reprinted from *Fear Knocks Presents*. Copyright © 2017 K. Scott Forman

"Erato," by K. Scott Forman: reprinted from *The Horror Writers Association presents Poetry Showcase Volume IV*. Copyright © 2017 K. S. Forman

"famille du jour," by K. Scott Forman; reprinted from *Fast Forward, Volume 2*. Copyright © 2009 K. Scott Forman

"Horseman," by K. Scott Forman; reprinted from *It Came from the Great Salt Lake: A Collection of Utah Horror*. Copyright © 2016 K. Scott Forman

"The House that Jack Built," by K. Scott Forman; reprinted from *Gothic Tales of Terror*. Copyright © 2015 K. Scott Forman

"Lost at Sea," by K. Scott Forman; reprinted from *Morpheus Tales, Issue 17*, and *Morpheus Tales: The Best Weird Fiction Volume 6*. Copyright © 2012, 2016 K. Scott Forman

"Lovecraft's Pillow," by K. Scott Forman: reprinted from *Fear Knocks Presents*. Copyright © 2017 K. Scott Forman

*The oldest and strongest emotion of mankind is fear,
and the oldest and strongest kind of fear is
fear of the unknown.*

Ph'nglui mglw'nafh Cthulhu R'lyeh wgah'nagl fhtagn

— *H.P. Lovecraft*

THE HOUSE THAT JACK BUILT

2 NOVEMBER 1898

Dear Nephew,

I tell you this tale in the hope that you will understand why I have isolated myself from your life, from the very commerce of mankind. I have hope that, once you have read my story, you will understand why I am the way I am, and why I do what I must do.

A thing I cannot explain haunts me. It hunts me in the cold dark streets and alleys of London, looks for me in the warm pubs of Whitechapel, and even watches me while I sleep. I write with the hope that no man or woman should suffer what I have suffered these many long years. These jots and tittles may seem the ravings of a madman, a lunatic, but they are true, as sure as I write them, and as sure as I breathe.

It was a decade ago, about this same time in early November. I found myself in the sorry state of rich knowledge and poor funds when I met the man who would become my benefactor, and my curse. Randolph Willard Rasmussen was infamous in circles unreachable to most. He was also the common man's friend. I had known of him, but this dark night we would become intimate.

I crossed paths with this aristocrat and knight, Sir Will as he was known to those of us in lesser circumstances, in an old pub in Whitechapel: the Ten Bells. Sir Will was wont to frequent pubs and taverns of each district in search of companionship and solace. He had a well-known condition – a troubled conscience, melancholy – that would crush even the most ardent in faith. Even those without scruples or moral compass would take pity on the man whilst he suffered from his condition.

I was gathering my writings and wondering where I would spend the night, or who would offer me work, when Will offered a round to the house. In my pauperized situation, I was more than willing to imbibe in a pint, as well as spend another hour with a roof over my head in relative warmth. I thanked the old gentleman, and soon, I found myself telling my story of misfortune to a man I wish I had never met.

My life had seemed the same for many months, and Will was empathetic. I was surprised at his understanding of the life of a writer, a constant student, scraping by on barely enough to eat, let alone, drink. The discussion continued into the more obscure literature, verging on alchemy and worlds beyond our own. I had written several pieces on other dimensions that had appeared in the rags around London, and was surprised that Will was familiar with them.

"I knew your grandfather, Martin, and I know your heritage."

His eyes fixed on mine as if we were more than acquaintances, as if some dark and secret knowledge bound us. I knew my heritage, more myth than material. Before I could question him, he changed the subject.

"What do you make of the recent killings?"

The question was valid, but unrelated to our ephemeral topics up to that point. The recent series of murders had left the police puzzled and without a suspect.

"Tragic," I said, "and inhuman."

"Yes," said Will.

I was taken for a moment by the passing shadow in Will's eyes, or pallor that appeared and disappeared on his face in the blink of an eye.

"Almost supernatural, as if—"

Sir Will paused, as if recalling something better left unspoken, and then continued.

"Natural or supernatural, forces indeed, that can take the life of a man or woman drop by drop. Do you feel it? A companion that hides in all humans, but only strikes when the time, the situation, allows, and when the stars are right."

I was struck by wonder, and then fear. My grandfather had said such things.

"Dark writing, myths and legends; I am accustomed to them, know them like history. They are—"

Will stopped, his eyes hard on my face. "They are something I know you, my friend, are very familiar with, although you pretend not to believe them."

He expressed a knowledge of some of my tales of the horrific, my cyclopean landscapes; he said they reminded him of Poe. His fascination with the macabre was troubling; his knowledge of things better left unspoken was impressive and disconcerting, but not as bewildering as his familiarity with me.

"Your fiction would be better if your facts were right, but then, who really knows the facts when it comes to the Dance of Death, or if one is trying to unlearn what he has learned?"

It was more a statement than a question. I wanted to ask how he knew who I was, who my family was, but he continued speaking of things terrible and sublime, arcane and distant. Then, the subject returned to the recent murders and the well-published writing of the fiend who had frequented the very district surrounding the pub in which we sat.

The Juwes are the men that will not be blamed for nothing.

"What do you make of that my well-read friend?" Will asked.

I was not prepared to respond. Certainly theories abounded of the murders: graffiti to put the police off the scent, simple anti-Semitism, or even Masonic secret knowledge linked to Hiram Abiff and the three ruffians that ended his life. There was no shortage of explanations, or of suspects.

"I was intrigued by the Masonic link, but I think it is probably just gibberish," I said.

"Isn't the Chief Superintendent a Mason? Arnold, isn't it?"

Sir Will eyed me, fire in his eyes, and then a sparkle, a glimmer of the promise of revelation. I broke the gaze and sipped my stout.

"You have heard the explanation of Juwes, but have you heard the murders have become a conspiracy? Protection extended from the highest levels of government to protect this madman and his family?"

I said nothing. Will continued.

"Those involved are the leaders of this nation, the very elite, the royals, who, by rights, should defend and protect even the most common street whore. Are the lights of Masonry involved, the money of the Jews, or is it all distraction from something grander and much more sinister?"

I had no response, although I was a curious listener to subjects of conspiracy and intrigue. Will's eyes revealed the kind of captive light created by sadness and the heft of the world on one's shoulders, the kind of light that a few pints had little effect on. At that moment I wished to reduce his burden.

"Look around. How many of these people can read, let alone see the subtleties of spelling? This was a message sent to those of us who grasp the deeper meaning of language."

"So," I said, "the Jews, the Masons, all subterfuge for something larger?"

"Larger, yes, and darker; no Jew or Mason has anything to do with it."

Will's tone was certain. He looked around as if someone might hear his voice. The sallowness of his skin changed, and I wondered if he had become unhinged.

"Are you feeling yourself this evening?" I asked.

"I've said too much as it is. I shan't say another word. It's not just me I'm worried about."

"What do you mean?" I asked.

Sir Will would not meet my eyes. Silently, we nursed our mugs to the dregs. I was curious, and I still felt compassion for this man, but my feelings were tempered with the understanding that men say things that mean nothing while under the influence of drink.

"I can feel his eyes upon me, lad. I know when he is near."

"What did you say?" I asked.

"I shall be blamed for nothing."

Will's countenance morphed to mad fear laced with anger. I waved for another round. Will swallowed in large gulps.

"Bring two more," said Will to the barkeep, "and a bottle of my medicine."

He drained the next pint in what seemed to be one large quaff. I sniffed the medicine bottle to find the sweet smells of scotch, but there was something more, something that hinted at a back room brew. Sir Will drank from the bottle; his composure seemed to return, which baffled me. The amount of spirits he had consumed in my presence alone would down a horse.

"Are you feeling better?" I asked.

"Tonight is the night. I can bear it no longer. I have watched you, Martin, for quite some time. Tonight, you have appeared to me, as if by the grace of God. I have a secret, and damn the thing, damn my life, damn it all for revealing it."

I was more than willing to hear my new found friend out, but something on the back of my neck, or deep in my bones, a conscience or a guardian angel, tried to warn me against it.

"Not here, not in this place," he said. "You must come with me; we will go to my study. I can tell you, I can show you. You must believe."

"Are you sure?"

"I'm not turning back. Tonight it ends for me."

He paused for a moment, looking in my eyes. An incredible sadness seemed to creep over his visage and I felt pity. Sir Will pitied me.

"I would not share this burden with any man unless he be willing. Martin, what I have to tell you will change you, could make you become like me. Are you sure you want to hear my tale?"

Again, the prick to flee and never look back, but my curiosity trumped any sense of safety.

"Let us be on our way."

"Good man, Martin."

The witching hour approached when we hailed a cab. We were soon in the warm study of Sir Randolph Willard Rasmussen; politician, philanthropist, and voice of the people. Will was as sober as a man could be, which troubled me. He hurried into a dim room and bade me sit in a comfortable chair facing its twin by the hearth. A fire burnt low. The servants had been dismissed.

Will returned, wiped his brow, looked toward the single window in the richly furnished apartment, and paced, first to the window, then to a bookcase, behind a large desk, and back to the door. I sat silently. Was I watching the fall of a pillar of society into the depths of madness? A clock chimed on a shelf near where I sat.

"Ah, fifteen minutes before midnight. The witching hour draws close. Are you ready, my friend, to hear my tale?"

I acknowledged my willingness. Will secured the lock on the window, drew the curtains, moved to the door, and locked it. He lit a lamp and placed it on a small table between the chairs. He then removed an old black volume from the bookcase, and sat down, placing the book on a small table between us. He opened the book, thumbed through several pages, and stopped, turning the book toward me.

"Do you recognize this drawing?"

I looked at a pentagram, upside down, the downward point aimed at a goat-headed image. I recognized the Eye of Horus at the seven o'clock point position, but the other three symbols at the inverted star's other points were unknown to me.

"Arcane occult symbology; I see the Egyptian, and this fellow must represent Pan, Satan, or whatever you please," I said, pointing at the bottom of the page.

"Yes. The other symbols come from a time and place you can only dream of. The Eye of Horus is our plane of existence, the goat the dark depths of Hell where all points fall. These other three represent other dimensions, other realms, complete with hidden knowledge, secrets, and powers of their own. Would you believe I've been to these places? Seen them? Brought back knowledge that made me what I am?"

I hardly believed a word Will said; although I was sure he believed it himself. I remained silent.

"You do not believe me, and you have long tried to forget the tales of your family. Tonight you will hear my tale and change your mind about a great many things. You will glimpse these places. You will witness my restitution for what I've done, for what I've covered up for so many months, and do what you were born to do. Did you know I had a twin, a brother?"

Will narrated a story of his youth; of a brother he loved dearly, his own ascent up the ladder of success in education and public service, his brother's descent into oblivion.

"My brother strayed from the family path, wasting time and talent studying the obscure arts lost to man, dabbling in sorcery and alchemy, looking for the philosopher's stone."

Where Will was a success in the light of day, his twin was a complete failure. Eventually, his brother disappeared, although he had been purposely forgotten by the family for many years. Will tried to maintain contact; the last word was his brother had fallen in with a bad lot and died in a den of iniquitous living in a faraway land. Will was devastated. Thus began his melancholy. He was lost without his brother.

"I didn't know what I would do. I spent several years mourning him, but then, last August, without any indication, my brother appeared at my door. He was well-groomed and looked every bit the gentleman in the dark light of night. I tried to embrace him, but he warned me not to touch him. He didn't want to contaminate me with the sickness he bore. I invited him in and he said nothing. I noticed a dark stain on his clothing."

Will's brother told a tale of travel, of discovery, and of losing his soul. He believed himself the servant of a dark power that demanded sacrifice. He had served this power, had been given a key that opened gateways to immense knowledge and sources of power. He did not weigh the cost, and now it was demanding payment. He had little self-control left. He asked Will to release him from his bondage, or else he would cease to exist as John Willard Rasmussen.

"What was I to do?" Will asked. "Who could believe such a story? Having just found my brother, was I to destroy him?"

The question had been asked before. I was remembering my history, tales long forgotten, and my grandfather. There was a king, a sister, an unholy union, and death. I shook my mind clear of the fable.

"What did you do?"

Will had fallen silent. He looked down at the book, then up at the clock. It was a few minutes until midnight.

"My brother had killed a woman."

"What woman?"

"One of the first of the recent killings on August 7, a Martha Tabrum."

I was shocked. I had read about it in the paper, remembered the name, but if this was true—

"My brother told me he was just obeying, but then the power seemed to seize him, consume him, and he feared the next victim would receive a much worse treatment. There would be more killings, payment for what he had got himself mixed up in."

"Your brother is this madman?"

Sir Will ignored the question. He looked at the curtained widow and then back at the book.

"My brother had killed before, but only those poor souls that were near death. It was compassion, a trade off, mercy given to the dying, deaths that would pay the price of his forbidden knowledge, but the evil demanded more, not just human lives, but human lives in their prime. My brother would have to continue killing until his debt was paid. He returned to London for my help, for sympathy at my hand. I didn't under- stand and asked him to explain."

Sir William looked at the book that still lay open before me.

"It was the last great secret, the secret to power and riches, the power to enter the forbidden realms, and it was never meant for man."

Its secrets came at a terrible price. Life was the payment for this forbidden knowledge, the life of the recipient, unless the recipient could provide substitutes. The book, the evil it contained, didn't care where payment came from, and the more life that was available, the more willing the book was to assist the debtor, to hide the crime, the sin, as well as open greater secrets, secrets that had similar costs, but it had all been a lie. The evil only needed a pathway into the human world.

There were rules, of course, even evil must obey rules. The killings continued. Will's connections in the constabulary, with the Masons and Jews, kept his likeness and his brother's off the suspect list. His brother's life was ruined. Will's would be next.

"Are you saying that you have something to do with the Ripper murders?" I asked.

"I did what I had to do. It was my own brother, but now his soul is lost in unknown realms, and his body is nothing but a shell for the evil he unloosed."

Will paused.

"I now know the horrible secret, and so do you."

He looked away, mumbling.

"Johnny, good old Jack…"

Sir Will was remembering the brother that had been, the brother that had left him in the grip of great sadness and remorse.

"My brother is gone and will never return, and I am already chosen as the next victim of this evil curse, the conduit between worlds."

This revelation was more than I could fathom. Will was either insane or the most practical man I had ever met.

The clock began to toll the midnight hour. The temperature chilled. Gooseflesh rose on my arms and legs. I looked about the room as the chimes struck one, two, three…

The lamp went out, the fire dimmed, the air dampened, and the putrid smell of decay filled my nostrils. I felt dizzy, grabbing onto the arms of the chair. The open book before me was the only object I could see clearly. Its pentagram blazed a bright orange, and then smoldered to red, then blue; it seemed to relax its light into a subtle green glow.

"The first time is unnerving."

I heard the voice, but it was distant, the sound bouncing off the sides of a metallic tube finally reaching my ears as hollow and empty. My vision remained clear, but only on the green light; the periphery was black and I had the sense that the darkness of Hell surrounded me.

"Whatever you do, do not let it touch your flesh."

The last words I would ever hear uttered from Will's lips.

The air I breathed sought exit from my lungs, from the room. The symbol turned yellow, then gold, then grew so bright I could not bear to look upon it. I closed my eyes and felt myself slip into darkness. The last chime struck twelve. All was silent, all was black.

A hand touched my shoulder. It was Will, but it wasn't Will. The man before me had Will's face, Will's clothes; he was Will as far as I could tell, but his eyes were not Will's eyes, and they filled like a slow pint with horror and hate. I pulled away.

"Where is Will?"

The thing that stood before me was gaunt, the skin pale and taut against the bones of its skull. Even in the dark light this man was clearly dead.

What had been horror and hate morphed to a blue burning light of evil at the back of the figure's eyes. Then I knew, this thing had been Will's brother, but was now something more, or less. What powers of darkness had wrought this transformation was beyond my comprehension. Here stood the man that Will believed to be his brother, his evil twin.

"I see recognition in your eyes," the figure said. "Will is trying to save himself and his brother, but he has only brought me another potential client. Are you planning to deal with me, Martin? I think you have a history of dealing with my kind. I can smell it in your blood."

I was speechless. This thing had caused terror to rain in blood through the streets of London, it wasn't a man, but something infinitely more evil and in the guise of a man, in the guise of Will's brother, John.

I felt the thing's thoughts, it had planned our meeting; its words, poison-laced with calmness and gentleness that unnerved, and who, I could only assume, believed we may become acquaintances, even friends.

"I think you may be different than my other acquisitions, but when you see what I have to offer, you will come to the same conclusion, or should I say, decision?"

The voice was mellow and comforting, but mixed with the sound of broken glass and metal grating against metal.

"No time for that now. We're off to the streets for some jolly fun."

He raised me as if by supernatural power, and before I knew where my legs were taking me, I found myself in a place with which I was unfamiliar. The trauma of the transformation and the late hour of night prevented me from getting my bearing. I was a victim of evil's pleasure.

"If you want to see Will alive, I have until the sun rises to complete my work. By then we must be back."

I was confused. The occult, the transmigration of souls, the rules of this dark game were lost on me. I was falling into a bottomless dream of darkness somewhere between reality and insanity. Whether in my body or out, the remainder of the hours of gloom and depravity became a blur.

I remember a room, a women; she was beautiful. But then I saw blood, more blood than I could imagine, and the wretched smell of evil and decay imprinted itself on my memory. The stench of the body's contents still overpowers all of my memories, all but one: the voice of John Willard Rasmussen.

"Sit down, my friend, and watch. You will come to enjoy this. Jack will have you back before you know it, and Bob's your uncle."

At some point, I must have fainted. I cannot remember leaving the scene. I awoke to the sound of a crackling fire. I felt as if I had been drinking all night. My skin was damp, a thin sheen of grime coated its surface, and a permanent chill had seeped into my bones. I recognized the room; had I ever left it?

What hideous atrocities transpired, what Providence had blocked from remembrance, I only could deduce from the papers the next day. I did not comprehend the vision. Had I witnessed the most brutal of murders, of rape and torture, or was it all just a nightmare?

Across from me sat Will, just as he had the night before. A pistol was in his hand and the angle of his head on his neck could only mean one thing. What had been Sir Randolph Willard Rasmussen was now the body of a self-destroyer.

I tried to get up, to flee, but I had no energy. I looked around. Only the book from the previous night lay within my grasp. It was closed, but a piece of paper hung from between its pages with my name written on its edge. I reached for it.

My friend, Martin, I see, too late I am afraid, that I have brought you into something I must end. I was weak when the evening began, hesitant. Now I must stop the madness. Take the book. The book is the key. I do not presume the danger has completely passed. I was my brother's connection to this world, and the connection to the evil he brought into it. That connection has been severed, as you see before you. I only hope I may find Jack on the other side of the Great Wall of Sleep.

There is a chance the evil may have connected to you, to your soul. I pray that you did not touch it, or allow it to touch you, and I pray you remember who you are. It consumed my brother, and has used me. I know who you are, or who you were, your family. You are the only one who could take this burden from me. Take every precaution; do not listen to it, the voices. It will speak to you in dreams, in visions, and when you least expect it. It anticipated I would stop its course, but it has been here before, it is an eternal evil, and it has alternatives.

What knowledge or power my brother may have gained, what secret combinations and blackmail his evil mentor planned to use against me, all are at an end. Forgive me if I have misjudged my actions, and for the position I have left you in.

I would ask you to find some way to destroy this book. I have failed. It will not yield to flame or acid, it will not remain hidden in the earth or at the bottom of the Thames. It was not fashioned on this earth, and I believe it can only be destroyed in the dimension from whence it came. Alas, I was unable to find the solution. Now the burden falls to you.

In a bag next to the table you will find several things to aid you. I have left a map to exit my estate unseen and undetected. You will find my signet ring. I have left instructions for a few trusted associates who are sworn to assist the bearer of my ring financially and will provide you with a large estate away from London. Good luck and God's speed.

Will signed and dated the letter 9 August 1888. A list of three names followed his signature. The killings stopped that night.

Since then, I have dreamed the same dream many times. I feel darkness creeping in occasionally, but I do not believe Will's brother, the vessel that contained the evil, has found his way back. It has been 10 years without incident. I know – don't ask me how – the evil is getting close again and is desperate. I feel its presence when I recall what I saw, and even when I'm not thinking about anything, just as Will said I would. I have written everything here, dear nephew, in case something happens to me, if I disappear, or if the murders begin again, so you alone will know the truth. If I am implicated in any kind of foul play, at least you will know I am guiltless.

I have the book and it has revealed its shallow promises, and much more. It knows my history, our history, and our role in stopping it centuries ago. I believe I've found a way to sever the link between this world and the others and plan to take the book out of this world. I do not know if I will be able to find my way back. If I fail, and the book remains in this realm, the task of keeping it safe will fall to you. I know my sister, your mother, has prepared for such a task, she has taught you the old ways, the ways of our fathers, of Merlin and Arthur.

I have left instructions with my solicitor. Upon my death, or my disappearance beyond three years, my estate falls to you. I pray that the book is not part of that estate and I find the key to excise this evil from our world. Remember your namesake. In you flows the blood of kings.

Sincerely and with love,
Your Uncle,
Martinus Uther Blacknight

MUMFORD'S GHOST

I FIND IT INTERESTING, REPULSIVE REALLY, WATCHING THE LATEST addition of mutants to the human gene pool at any large bargain store. It adds a forced frugality: the distractions and images quickly quell the desire to purchase anything. I have yet to see a mutant of superhero stock at any of these outlets of excess and gluttony, and I doubt I ever will, especially after the day I saw Mumford's ghost.

I walked the aisles that day, like a voyeur in a B-movie, the reason for my visit forgotten in folds of flesh and inbreeding that surrounded me. An environment where one can buy a lifetime supply of fish oil or laundry detergent is a magnet for creatures that touch all of the senses, not just sight, and soon one is lost in a cavalcade of horror almost touching the sublime. To describe the ocean of unsupported flesh, cleavage in all its varieties knowing no gender, age, or ethnicity, combined with the mass aroma culled from bodies of the undisciplined and morbidly obese is truth stranger than truth.

I considered returning to my car. A gentle warning sounded in my subconscious. If I stayed I would be unofficially tasked to judge the bargain behemoth's Plumber Crack of the Day Contest, which as of this writing has become a coed event. I turned to leave, but contestants had already started to enter the runways of aisles displaying their wares. I was trapped.

Most were single entrants, but sometimes two or three from the same gene pool would make eye contact; a disturbing daddy-daughter date

Deliverance-style candidate looked to be a clear winner, but there were plenty of husband-wife *can you believe we have children* contenders. Most must have had their brood, all eight in tow, when they were 100 pounds younger and still confused about the results of rutting. I found myself missing the safety of being a stay-at-home introvert when it comes to shopping and wished for the protection of my wife.

I heeded the inner voice and headed back the way I had come, but aisle after aisle of contestants shining light from a hill of gluttony, a well-lit beacon that no mere bushel could ever conceal, hypnotized me and I was lost. I looked at the floor. I remembered the room of mirrors at amusement parks and the floor would always guide one out of optical illusions. It almost worked. Something stopped me.

A noise, or a smell, probably both, washed over me and my eyes involuntarily left the floor. I was on the cookie and candy aisle. A woman who would soon bear the title *Crack Queen of the Day* blocked my way. Then I saw him. Mumford.

I blinked, shook my head, tried to clear my lungs of imagined excess and excrement in the air. It just couldn't be. Mumford was dead, a murky memory, one I had tried to forget, or at least never thought about on purpose. The questions that always popped into my mind about Mumford returned. Why did he marry Sharon and how could he father children with her? It was a mystery, a physical impossibility or maybe just mental and emotional revulsion culling questions from my dark heart that should never have answers. Then the third and final question: did Sharon push him over the edge?

Mumford was a case of the Modern Prometheus gone awry, if such a thing was possible, and at the funeral I could finally understand why Victor Frankenstein, in his one and only moment of courage, destroyed his creation's mate. It would lead to mutants shopping at volume discount stores, it would lead to excess and gluttony, and it would lead to more Sharons. The theme continued in my mind, the questions repeating with answers. The only body fluid cocktail that Mumford or his wife could mix involved sweat and saliva. The cabbage patch or the stork was the only plausible means of delivery for their offspring. Then it hit me again. Mumford was dead.

I looked up and could only see the woman, or what was once a woman. Maybe it was her likeness to Sharon that had caused my hallucination? Mumford had never been there at all. I had imagined it. The fetid smell of trailers and cheap food whispering from the pores of the potato chip diet brigade was affecting my vision. The woman that blocked my way brought the memory of Mumford back and his wife.

Sharon Mumford could not be classified on such superficial scales of measurement as beauty or even girth. She was obese, leaning toward the red-line on that gauge, but that measurement didn't really speak to her surface area or lack of good looks. It was the things not easily visible, the things that explain how people find love and have children or discover hate and divorce that made her tick. I never could understand what Mumford saw in her, or smelled in her, but what made her tick became a time bomb that led him to a final solution.

I hasten to use Stevenson's term: *self-destroyer*. Suicide is rather bland in describing what happened to Mumford. No one really can understand it, its fleeting nature, or how under-rated it can be. Self-destroyer makes it sound so purposeful. Mental health professionals don't make it any better or easier to understand, and in the end, at least in the case of Mumford, self-destroyer, would only elevate and elicit empathy. I prefer another term, a poor man's time machine, but like most things that go against nature, the operations of such an idea can go awry.

There were rumors of auto-asphyxiation. I believed Mumford wanted to travel in time, but not to multiple locations, just a single destination, and only for short respites. In retrospect, I think the emotion altered the settings on his machine. The joy of escape overcame him like the thinking of a mad zealot. He thought he was in control and didn't need to know how to land until it was too late.

A smell that was becoming familiar brought me back to reality, the candy aisle, and the woman. The only evidence that any time had passed was the amount of junk food that filled her cart. I started to turn around, to take a detour around the Queen, but then it happened again. An image, silver, threads blinking on and off, and then Mumford materialized.

Pain made me blink. My jaw had dropped further than it should have. I closed my mouth, blinked again, and this time he wasn't gone. He flickered in the air, a specter, and I wanted to speak, but couldn't. I was having difficulty even breathing, and when I could speak, he disappeared again.

I thought I was going crazy, but instead of reason, all the conclusions that people have in situations like this, all the deduced explanations, washed over me. Then I thought about why. Why would Mumford be a ghost and why would he be at discount store?

Mental health offers palatable explanations that never decompose completely in the graveyards of our minds. Religion, with all its horror and black and white answers, is often a much better alternative, but in this case I could only think of Dickens. Mumford's selfish act, according to religion, and my hallucinations, mental health, could be explained by undigested meat or underdone potatoes.

I felt like a dog chasing his tail, no real answers or resolutions. The funeral, the events leading up to it, all had unsatisfying answers that never answered the questions on everyone's lips: what really happened? Mumford's exit from this plane of existence to another was a story that needed to be read in those around him, rewritten and reread before one could understand the real story. I always believed it was the things not visible in Sharon that led to Mumford's departure, not suicide. He confused time travel with space travel: a one-way ticket, destination unknown, and instead of a temporary visit he stranded himself on a seldom visited planet. Something went wrong.

The exact cause of death was unclear, or at least unspoken, but the erotic asphyxiation gone wrong explanation was the most interesting, if not the most entertaining and plausible. It was a good horror movie, engaging and repulsive at the same time. Of course, this rumor was never openly discussed, especially at the funeral, but in my mind the fiction of rumor clearly pointed to the non-fiction of Sharon Mumford.

I could picture Mumford as a gasper: paraphilia fit him like a rubber glove. The act, they say, is as powerful as a cocaine high and just as addicting. Mumford needed to get high, at least high above the mundane existence he had with Sharon. Perhaps paraphilia was a transitory relief from his ample wife, a potent high that could transport him to an alternate reality alone. It would have given him a breather and maybe enabled him to live through the days and nights with Sharon.

I felt better about Mumford thinking it was true, but now, seeing his ghost, I wasn't so sure.

There were other clues: Mumford had lived beyond his means, he was a nerd-geek hybrid with weird and expensive tastes, Sharon's appetite alone would require a man to work several jobs to keep her nourished, and then there were the eight children, all carbon copies of Sharon. A monthly house payment and all other debts aside, Mumford was Prometheus's liver every payday, but instead of one organ, Sharon swooped down and devoured them all. That could lead one to choices, to an escape plan, especially one with unknown consequences rarely considered.

I focused on the spot I had seen Mumford. The store, the fluorescent lights, I must have been getting a migraine. Maybe it was my undiagnosed PTSD from the war, from the wars, manifesting in a ghost. Why was it Mumford's ghost? I closed my eyes. The funeral appeared.

Colleagues, friends, and family; the service was common and the preacher avoided the cause of death. He laced his sermon with the many promises of an afterlife, the reflections of what a good guy Mumford was, and how tragic it all was, especially for the family. I didn't believe the preacher, or that Mumford was a good guy. Sharon was the real tragedy. She was more abysmal than the sermon or anything Mumford ever did. I watched her and the children. I didn't see tragedy in their faces. I saw impatience and sweat. A luncheon was to follow the service.

I remember suppressing a laugh. Sharon would starve to death without a steady flow of income and charity. Perhaps she had already planned to eat her own children if it came to that. An image of an obese woman who had lost her cat came to mind. As the woman turns, the observer sees the cat stuck in the woman's crack. I could see one or two of Mumford's children ending up that way. I could even hear a meow.

A squeaky wheel on the woman's cart was the meow, and I was back on the aisle. She had turned. A crack the size of the San Andres stared back at me. No cats or children.

What had I seen? The woman blocked my forward progress. Her width reached from the cookies and crackers on the right of the aisle to the cakes and doughnuts on the left. I thought about the thousands of hours of self-indulgence that went into that body, and then sickened at the tens of thousands, even millions, of innocent beads of sweat trapped in the folds of this cellulite princess's gelatinous flab. I was about to turn again. Mumford appeared, but this time he looked at me.

A chemical reaction simultaneously occurred in my throat, stomach, and bowels, an equal and opposite reaction to the woman's eau de toilette. It must have triggered my inner eye, something on a metaphysical level. He was the same silver specter, but I saw something else. His spirit was tethered at the very peak of this woman's rear fissure almost like a cartoon balloon of dialogue waiting to emit a sound described in smell. His eyes registered instant recognition. Mumford still had the geeky grin, the face that reminded me of a happy rat, the nose that moved like a mouse nearing cheese. I mouthed his name and his eyes lit up. I was obviously the first mortal to see him or attempt communication.

His ghost lips moved, but I couldn't hear anything. I started to approach, to see if communication was possible, but the Countess of

Crevice ambled around, facing me, and Mumford followed her crack. Her frame fondled itself in single shudders with each step as she started toward me. It was like an ocean wave, a tsunami, crashing against the shore with each drop of her foot on the innocent floor. The imagined shock wave hit me, the eureka effect, the terror that now keeps me away from big bargain stores, the truth.

I saw Marley and the chains he had forged in life in Mumford, but instead of chains, I saw flesh. The punishment for his act was far more horrendous and horrid than the act itself: condemned to a life of confinement, incarceration, tied to this thing. It was inhumane and extraordinary in its simplicity and sublimity, but then it got worse. I recognized the woman. I was staring at Mumford's ball and chain.

"Sharon?"

The mass looked up, the syllables of the name familiar, but the memory that the name belonged to her temporarily lost in an empty carbohydrate haze. She blinked.

"Sharon Mumford?" I repeated.

Her gaze waivered and blinked into a feral intensity, possibly insulin shock, and then her eyes clouded into cotton candy. Whatever was lost in memory was also lost in speech. With a great effort, the mass that had been a human being backed away from me, quivered in a single, slow rotation, and resumed a new course back the way it had come. The silver strands of Mumford's ghost flashed like a blinking traffic signal, his spiritual fabric disappearing and reappearing, fettered to the single point that had only moments before secured Sharon's victory in my imaginary butt cleavage contest.

"Mumford," I whispered.

There was no reply. Silver tears rained to the hard floor, striking and shattering into invisible sorrows. I could only wave goodbye.

I never saw Mumford again. I avoid super stores and women that have cleavage in more than one place. Mumford's decision didn't end it all, it only prolonged it, and cemented his destiny to that which he desired the most to escape. No religion or mental health manual could explain what happened.

I try not to think about it, or Mumford. The dead are among us, but they do not travel fast. I do take some pleasure in knowing Sharon will suffer a similar fate. Sloth isn't a normal means of suicide, nor is it quick or painless, but those who chose it usually succeed on the first attempt.

NEIGHBOR OF THE BEAST

It was in the summer of 1999, I took a room in a large apartment complex that stood a few minutes' walk from my first job. I had just graduated Magna Cum Average, the job was entry level at an inner-city high school, and my rooms were Spartan to say the least. On a high school teacher's wages it was comfortable, and it was more than just a room and a hotplate: one bedroom, one bath, and a small living room and kitchen combo. The place had a faint odor that I could never quite put my finger on, but when it rained it smelled like burnt matches, sulphur.

The other tenants were a quiet bunch, not overtly friendly or unfriendly, but apathetic. They reminded me of the majority of voters: they had an opinion about every topic when given a chance to talk, but when asked what they would do, no action followed.

There was Mrs. Fizzle next to me; an older widow in 669 whose life seemed to revolve around her cat. Mr. Crowley was across from her in 668. He was a divorcee, an avowed woman-hater, who worked long hours somewhere downtown in a job that nobody could determine. The Pratts were on my other side, a young couple in 665 with a new baby, who had every intention, I believe, of becoming an opera singer or an umpire, based on his lung capacity. Across from them in 664 were a couple of girls, Sandra and Jalene, working their way through college and splitting the rent.

I really didn't hit it off with any of them, but was cordial when we would pass in the hall. If I happened to run into one of them downtown, which rarely happened, I was courteous. To tell the truth, I avoided them.

Then there was the tenant in 666. He intrigued me.

Like me, he avoided people, and when he couldn't avoid them he looked at his feet to avoid eye contact. He rarely left his apartment. He wasn't a bad sort; in fact, he was rather handsome and looked to me as having great potential with the ladies. He always wore amazing business attire – an immaculately white pressed shirt underneath an immaculately tailored dark suit, usually black, with an immaculate silk tie, also black. On occasion there was a subtle splash of red in his tie. It was on just such a day that I greeted him for the first time.

"Hello, neighbor. I noticed you have some red in your tie today."

At first, 666 acted a little surprised, then put out, then annoyed, and finally, after making eye contact, he said, "I'm sorry, you're the new fellow in 667."

I acknowledged his observation.

"Yes, some days I go a little crazy and add a little excitement to my life," he said.

I was taken aback for a moment by the change from irritation to genuine warmth and civility in only a single sentence. For one who would go to great lengths to avoid his neighbors, Mr. 666 was quite personable and engaging.

"You must be very busy. I've only seen you a few times, and didn't get a chance to introduce myself properly. I'm Adam West."

There was a visible cringe at the mention of my name, but he recovered quickly.

"Like the Batman actor?"

"Yes, I'm afraid so."

"It's good to meet you, Adam." He cringed again speaking my name, but reached out and shook my hand just the same. "I would like to chat longer, but I'm quite busy. Perhaps I can invite you for a coffee sometime?"

"That would be nice."

And without another word, or his name, 666 disappeared behind the door with his namesake in dull gold numerals below the peephole. I was left standing alone in the corridor.

Several weeks passed and Mr. 666 was invisible. For all I could tell, I was the last person to see him alive. Then, one evening after a particularly hard day at work, there was a knock on my door.

"Hello, Ad…, Mr. West. I just finished work and remembered I had invited you for coffee. Is it a bad time?"

He still had a problem saying my name, but at least he remembered it.

"No, not at all. I've just had a terrible day at work and a break with an adult would be nice."

"Why don't you get your coat, and we'll go down to the coffee shop on the corner?"

I invited him in, still not knowing his name, got my jacket, and we were on our way.

"I don't believe I ever got your name."

"Oh, I'm sorry. You can call me Joshua. Joshua Caine."

It seemed like a normal enough name, but just didn't fit my neighbor for some reason. It was like a sixth sense was going off in my head somewhere. We continued out of the apartment complex and were soon enjoying a good cup of coffee and conversation.

"So a hard day at the office, Adam?"

"You could say that; 35 teenagers who seem to have never learned how to think, or read, for that matter."

"You're a school teacher? What a grand profession."

I wasn't feeling grand at the moment.

"It wasn't like that when I was a kid," said Joshua, "teachers were God back then."

"It's too bad that isn't the case anymore," I said. "I think teachers have become one of the lowest life-forms on the planet."

Joshua just smiled. He sipped his coffee and replied, "Maybe, Adam, but a necessary life-form."

Joshua appeared to be having less trouble saying my name, but there was still something in his eyes that betrayed his difficulty.

"So what do you do, Joshua?"

"As little as possible," he laughed. It was a warm and inviting laugh that I couldn't help myself in joining.

"No, seriously."

"Seriously?"

He paused and a twinkle appeared in his eyes.

"Let's just say I play the market. You know the old saying: *he who has the gold makes the rules*."

His smile was as contagious as his laugh, and I returned it, but waited for a more specific answer.

"I guess you could say I'm a day-trader."

"That would explain why I don't see you that often."

"Yes, I'm afraid I'm glued to my computer screens from dawn to dusk."

"You appear to have been very successful at it. Why do you continue to stay in your apartment? If it's anything like mine it's got to be a hole."

"I guess I just don't like change, and the rent is reasonable."

"I guess frugality would come in handy for someone who is into making money, not spending it."

He laughed again and then smiled.

"You know, Adam, you're rather likeable. Perhaps I'll give you a tip that will allow you to move out of the DeVille."

"The DeVille?"

"That's the name of our apartment complex. You probably didn't know that, did you?"

"Sounds like that woman in the Disney movie."

He laughed again. "Yes, it does, doesn't it?"

He was silent for a moment and then continued.

"When I moved into the DeVille, it was brand new. That must have been back in 1966."

"You've been here for over 30 years?"

"Sure. It's a nice place, the neighborhood is quiet, and the tenants aren't a bad sort. It's also close to the business district. Remember, in those days the Internet and personal home computers were the stuff of science fiction."

"I guess you're right. So you had a seat on the exchange?"

"The exchange." He smiled and looked into his coffee. "I guess you could call it that."

I was curious. I wondered how much money my neighbor was making, but didn't think it proper to ask."

"$250,000."

"What?"

"The amount of money I'm making. You were thinking it, weren't you?"

"I was curious, I guess. So, $250,000 a year. That's not a bad figure."

He was smiling.

"What?"

"That's how much I make on average."

He paused again.

"Per day, per client."

I was shocked, but quickly regained my composure.

"So I guess you're buying the coffee?"

He laughed again.

It was several weeks before I saw Joshua again. He was wearing a red tie this time.

"Must be a great day for you to wear a tie like that."

"Oh, hello, Adam. I must apologize for not coming by more often. I've just been busy."

"Don't worry about it. I understand. Me too."

"Yes, you have been busy too. Let me check my messages, and then perhaps a cup of coffee? Your turn to buy."

He smiled and I felt all the cares of the school day go away.

"How can I refuse an offer like that? Let me get my coat."

Soon we were chatting again as if the intervening weeks were only a day. I was really getting to like my neighbor.

"So, I guess college wasn't cheap. Did you have to take out many loans?"

"Don't remind me." Joshua was smiling at me. "As a matter of fact, I managed to work my way through most of college. I'm only in about $15,000. Some of my classmates are into it $40,000 or more."

"That's too bad. Even $15,000 is a large number. I wish there was some way I could help, Adam. I'm starting to like you."

"I wish there was a way you could help too, but I'm sure I'll be able to manage, as long as you keep buying the coffee."

Joshua laughed, and then he grew more serious.

"How much liquid cash do you have lying around, Adam?"

"You're kidding, right? Let me see." I reached into my pocket. "Looks like ten dollars and 35, no, 45 cents."

"No, I'm serious. How much money could you get your hands on, say, by Thursday?"

"The day after tomorrow?"

"Yes, the day after tomorrow."

Joshua was serious. Not a serious that frightens, but a serious that means a serious answer is warranted.

"I guess I have a few hundred in saving, a few hundred in checking. I could probably get around $1,000."

"Good. That should just about do it. I have a hot tip for you."

"But I don't even have a stockbroker."

"That is a problem."

He thought for a minute, but his eyes betrayed him. He already seemed to know how this was going to go down.

"Adam, I know you don't really know me, but…"

"…but I could give it to you, and you could invest it for me."

"Yes, something like that. Oh, that would never work. After all, we've only met for coffee twice, passed each other in the hall a few times."

I knew he was right, but at the same time I knew he wouldn't cheat me. Some feeling came over me that convinced me this was the right thing to do.

"I'll bring it by Thursday evening, if that will be okay?"

"Wonderful. I'm sure you will be very happy with the results."

Thursday came and went, as did Friday and Saturday. No Joshua. Perhaps I was a little too trusting, after all he had a trusting face, impeccable clothes and manners, and everything about him made me think trust. At the same time, I didn't want to go knocking on his door. I didn't want to convey I didn't trust him, but the seed of doubt had been planted. I made the decision to go over first thing Sunday morning.

I felt funny, felt kind of foolish, and even turned around and went back into my rooms a couple of times. After all, I had to show some kind of trust. Maybe he had to go on a business trip, maybe something came up, or maybe he was in an accident. Finally, I had to know. I opened my door and–

"Adam! What a pleasant surprise. I was just on my way over to your place. I must apologize for not contacting you sooner. You must have thought I had taken your life savings and skipped town."

I mumbled a few words of denial, but I knew he could read my thoughts.

"Good news. It looks like you're dressed. Let's go get a cup of coffee and I'll fill you in on your investment."

Soon I was drinking a large café latte and Joshua was drinking his usual triple espresso.

"I'm sorry I didn't have time to get cash, so I hope you don't mind this cashier's check. The name is spelled correctly?"

I looked at the check: Pay to the Order of: Adam West. Everything looked fine until I read the amount: $17,506.66.

"This can't be."

The words hung in the air as I felt my mouth drop open and freeze, the room froze, everything froze. $17,506.66.

"I expected a little more, but with broker fees and everything, it's the best we could do."

"I can't take this, Joshua. I can't take this money. I didn't do anything to earn it."

"Sure you did, Adam. You did a lot more than most. You put your trust in someone who then put your money to work for you. People have been doing this since the beginning of time. Remember the guys and the talents in the Bible? Let's just say you gave this servant 1,000 talents and he returned you 16,506.66 talents."

Joshua was smiling. His eyes were twinkling. I couldn't help feeling all warm inside.

"Thank you. I don't know what else to say. I owe you big time."

"That's the spirit. You are most welcome, and you don't owe me anything. You already paid me ten-fold in your trust. It's been a long time since anyone has really trusted me, let alone acted like a friend. Besides, I took my cut. Nothing is free in this world."

"Thank you," I said.

It was interesting watching Joshua's reaction. It seemed that he had not heard those two words in a long time.

"I did take ten percent, Adam."

"I would have been more than happy just to have doubled my money, Joshua. You don't know what this means."

Joshua looked nostalgic, sitting there with his smile, starring out the window at passerby. I don't remember what else was said that day, but I do remember sending in a check for $14,988.26 the next day to erase my student loans. I didn't really know what to do, to think, to even say. Was it Fate, Destiny, Luck, that brought me in contact with Joshua? All I knew was that I would forever be in grateful debt to the kindness of my neighbor in room 666.

A few months passed. I would see Joshua about twice a month and we would always go for coffee. I had a feeling that Joshua was lonely, that he had no family, although he would never admit it and I would never ask. I did ask him about my name, which seemed to be bothering him less when he said it. He laughed and admitted to having an old friend named Adam; they had a falling out, went their separate ways, and then Adam had passed away. Joshua regretted never making things right between them.

"We had been very close, like brothers."

Our friendship seemed to give him great pleasure. He never offered another stock tip, and I never asked. We had something, the two of us, something that couldn't be put into words.

"You know, Adam, I was sincere about you owing me nothing."

Suddenly, I felt a little chill. I felt like the moment had come where I would have to pay the piper, or the reaper. Again, it was as if he could read my mind.

"No, Adam, it's nothing like that. I would never ask you to do something. I just want you to avoid a certain situation."

I was confused. I didn't know what he was going to ask me to do.

"You know that cute little blonde in your third period. Missy I think her name is."

"How do you know about my students?"

I was getting a little scared. Suddenly, the man I had started to consider a second father was aware of my personal life, or at least my personal profession.

"Adam, don't worry. I'm not spying on you, but I have friends, acquaintances really, in obscure places, people that know things, that keep tabs on my investments."

"Am I an investment?"

"No, no, not at all. I just have an acquaintance in the school district, I mentioned your name in passing as a friend, and he remembered and called me the other day."

"Who?"

"I really can't say, business and everything, you understand?"

I didn't understand, but he continued.

"Let me just warn you to stay away from her. I know you are a wonderful teacher, and you would never do anything wrong, but that doesn't stop other people from doing things that are wrong, or that can affect others."

"What are you saying?"

"Missy is going to get you into a world of trouble if you don't avoid her."

"How do I avoid a student?"

"Not in class, Adam, but when you're out of class."

"How do you know this? What are you saying?"

"You'll just have to trust me, Adam. I don't want to see you get into trouble, and I really can't tell you anything else. Confidentiality and all."

"You know about my students. What else do you know about me?"

"Adam, we're friends. I don't purposely snoop into your life, just as you haven't snooped into mine. We trust one another. Let's just say it was fortuitous that I mentioned your name in passing to an associate and he was kind enough to advise me to warn you. Can we just leave it at that?"

Things had changed. I felt violated, although I wouldn't say as much. The man who had helped me greatly - had been my only real friend in the city - was now something other than what I expected, or so I thought. Maybe I should find out who Joshua Caine really was.

The week started and I was a little jumpy when third period came around. I couldn't help notice that Missy was watching me more than ever, but I convinced myself that I was imagining things. It was Joshua that had put that in my mind.

After class I had my preparation period. The words that Joshua said still haunted me. *You'll just have to trust me.* I took some papers I needed to grade and headed for the teachers' lounge. There would be a few teachers in there I knew, and despite wanting to not believe anything Joshua had said, I couldn't take a chance.

It was Wednesday when it happened. Missy stayed after class.

"Mr. West, I've been trying to meet with you after class all week. Do you have some time we could talk?"

"Sure, Missy. What about?"

"Could we go to your office? I need some privacy."

All the bells and whistles were suddenly going off in my head. This was the moment Joshua had warned me about.

"Actually, I'm meeting Mr. Franks right now, Missy. Would you mind talking to me in the teachers' lounge?"

"I kind of wanted to be alone with you."

Missy was coming on to me. She was actually doing a slight shimmy, and wetting her lips, even as the last of the students were leaving the classroom.

"I'm sorry, Missy, perhaps we can meet after school. I'm sure we can talk in one of the counselors' offices."

"But I need to talk to you now, and not in public."

This girl was in heat. I didn't know why, and didn't want to know why, but one thing was for sure: I had to avoid Missy at all costs.

"I'm sorry, Missy, but it will just have to be later."

"Maybe after school then?"

I had my briefcase packed and my coat on before the final bell rang and was long gone before anyone was the wiser. I was scared, and not of Missy. Where did Joshua get his information? Did he have some connection to the CIA or FBI? Maybe the Mafia? Was the money that he had made for me blood money? I had to talk to him. I wasn't about to snoop around behind his back.

Joshua was not home, nor was he home for the rest of the week. At the same time, Missy was more intent on getting me alone. I actually asked a co-worker to come by and get me after third period on Thursday and Friday. What was going on, and for how long did I have to avoid her. It was Saturday evening when things got really out of control.

"Mr. West, I'm coming over to your apartment right now."

"Missy?"

"I need to see you."

"Missy, how did you get my phone number? How do you know where I live?"

"Don't leave. I'm coming over right now."

"Missy? Missy!"

I was in trouble. I didn't know what to do. I grabbed my coat and keys and ran out the door into the hall. Looking both ways, I didn't know whether to take the stairs or the elevator. The elevator bell rang. The doors were opening. What now?

It was Joshua, and he was alone. He was walking with his eyes to the floor as usual.

"Joshua! Thank God you're here!"

He looked up, his eyes seemed to radiate pure evil, but his countenance changed immediately when he saw it was me.

"Adam! What seems to be the trouble?"

"I took your advice about Missy, and she's been after me this whole week. She's coming up here right now and I have nowhere to go."

"My, isn't she a persistent one. I could use somebody like her in acquisitions."

"What?"

"Oh, I'm sorry. I guess you better make a run for the fire-escape, she'll certainly take the elevator."

"What?"

"I guess I could let you lie low in my place for a while."

"Thank you, Joshua, thank you very much."

And with that I followed him into his apartment.

The shock of the spaciousness of the entry and living room made me forget my troubles for a minute.

"Wow!"

"It's quite humble, actually, but I call it home."

Joshua removed his overcoat and then appeared to think.

"Perhaps you should lend me your key and we'll give Missy a surprise."

For a moment I didn't know what Joshua meant.

"I'll be the tenant in 667."

"That's a good idea!"

He was gone with my key before I could say anything else. I was left standing in the entry, which was nicely paneled and had a very nice picture over a library table. The picture almost looked alive and reminded me of something I had seen before. It was the picture of Dorian Gray, and it seemed to be watching me. I stepped into the living room leaving Dorian's gaze on my back.

The room was actually the same size as mine, but the way it was furnished made it look much larger. The couches and chair were covered in fine leather, the coffee table, and various stands were made of a dark wood that seemed to be rather heavy and antique. Various pieces of art hung from the walls, all from famous painters, but what drew my attention was a large bookcase with glass doors opposite the kitchen and bedroom.

I looked through the glass and saw books bound in leather and other coverings that looked like they had come from another century, or even millennium. Despite the look of antiquity, they appeared almost new. Paradise Lost by Milton, Faust by Goethe, and the Screwtape Letters by C. S. Lewis were the first ones I recognized. Surely, many of the classics of English literature adorned these shelves, and I was not surprised to see Dickens, Shakespeare, and even my friend from the entry, Oscar Wilde's the Picture of Dorian Gray. As I gazed over the shelves, titles that I didn't expect my friend to enjoy were there: Frankenstein by Shelley, Dracula by Stoker, and Jekyll and Hyde by Stevenson were companions with the H. P. Lovecraft and even Stephen King. As I got to the last column of shelves there were several Bibles, works of philosophy and religion, including Plato and Freud, Mohammed and Zoroaster, but the biggest surprise was a collection of the Romantic Poets: Blake, Coleridge, Shelley, Byron, and others.

"I see you have found my favorites, Adam. Nothing like a good poem about free love, or good and evil, or existential thought to get the heart pumping."

"I didn't hear you come in."

"Sorry about that. I didn't mean to startle you. Speaking of startle, I don't think Missy will be back."

"What do you mean?"

The twinkle in his eye was back. "Let's just say she didn't want to be my escort for the evening." He laughed out loud.

"I hope you're right."

He had composed himself. "So, do you like good literature, Adam?"

"I minored in English, so I'm familiar with most of these titles. This is an amazing collection. Some of these look like first editions."

"They all are first editions."

"Even the Bible."

He laughed again. "I wouldn't exactly say it was what the prophets and apostles wrote down, nor is it autographed, but it did come off the Gutenberg press."

I didn't know if I should laugh, or if I should just believe him.

"In fact, most of them, other than the Bible and some of the older works, have been signed by the authors. My particular favorite is The Scarlet Letter."

"Hawthorne?"

"Yes."

"That's unbelievable."

"Well, I do have one weakness. I love original works of art, whether they be literature, painting, sculpture."

"So are these painting authentic?"

"Yes, they are the originals."

I looked again. I wasn't very knowledgeable about art, but I had seen all the pieces before.

"Monet, Manet, Renoir, Gauguin – I also have a nice piece by Rodin over by the kitchen, but I'm particularly fond of this piece by Da Vinci."

Joshua was holding what looked like a small version of Da Vinci's horse carved in Onyx. His eyes appeared misty.

"I remember when he gave me this. It seemed so long ago. I'm sorry, Adam. You must think me delusional."

"No, not at all."

Delusional? No. Crazy? I was beginning to wonder.

"I know how some things can really hold emotional value. I have something, not a famous work of art or anything, but an object that holds great value to me," I said.

"Really? Something from your childhood, perhaps something from a parent?"

"As a matter of fact, yes. My father gave me his own pocketknife when I was 8 years old. I have always kept it with me."

I placed my hand in my pocket and felt the small, well-worn knife, and pulled it out.

"I take it your father is no longer with us."

"No, he died when I was 12."

"I'm sorry, Adam. I'm glad you have something nice to remember him by. Sometimes I wish I had something to remember my father by, but it usually passes."

We stood for a moment in silence. I could only imagine what Joshua was thinking, or feeling.

"Well, I appreciate your hospitality, and helping me out of a jam. I best be going. Thank you."

"You're welcome, Adam. I think that this particular problem is solved."

As I started to leave I spoke. "Joshua, how did you know about Missy? What trouble did you see happening?"

"I can't really say. Perhaps I can tell you more at a later time. Maybe over coffee next week."

"It's just that I don't know what to think about you anymore. Are you some kind of spy, working for the mob, a CIA operative, what?"

He laughed and the sparkle was back in his eye.

"All those things and more, Adam. I'll have to tell you about it over coffee next time."

He placed his hand on my shoulder and guided me to the door. We parted like old friends and I didn't pursue the question. It would be impolite and impertinent after the kindness my neighbor had already shown. I left him smiling at me in his doorway.

A week passed, I ran into Joshua several times, but he was always in a hurry. Finally, after a few more weeks passed, he came by, apologized for not talking more often, and invited me out for our habitual coffee and chitchat.

"So, your first year teaching is winding down. What do you have, six or eight weeks left?"

"Seven weeks, but exactly 30 working days with holidays and breaks included."

"Do you have it figured down to the hours?"

"Does my excitement over summer break show that much?"

"I'm afraid it does."

"I know I may sound negative, or burned out, but I really like the job. It's just…"

"Not as rewarding as you thought it would be?"

"Yes, something like that. I thought if I only could reach one student, it would all be worth it, but I don't think I reached any this year, especially Missy."

"Yes, it was too bad about her pregnancy and the gym coach."

I looked up. He was smiling, and then laughed out loud."

"I guess it's okay to tell you now. The gym coach was, emphasis on was, one of my clients. I found out about his extracurricular activities, his tactics, and I believed he was planning to get you in the sack with Missy and–"

"And my career as a teacher would have been over."

"That's about the long and short of it."

"I don't understand how he could have been one of your clients. He doesn't make much more than I do."

"Let's just say he owed me some money, which he was unable to pay. The revelation of Missy and his other sorted past activities was part of the price he had to pay."

"What do you mean?"

"I know this is going to sound quite terrible, but when I have clients who do not keep their commitments I sometimes must resort to other means to extract payment."

"But how could you have gained anything from revealing his bad behavior?"

"It's not all about money, Adam. I don't think you really understand what I do for a living."

"I guess I don't."

"You're the first friend I've had in a long, long time. Can I call you my friend?"

"I think after all you've done for me, I should be calling you my friend."

"I don't expect you to believe any of this, but I like you, Adam."

He paused, smiled, and then continued.

"When I said I was a day trader I'm sure you thought I traded in stocks. My little investment of your money probably only added to that half-truth."

Joshua paused and looked at me intently. I could tell he really wanted me to believe him.

"I actually trade in souls."

"Well, based on your story of the gym coach, I can believe it, but what about the $250,000 per day? You can't really make that kind of money trading in souls."

"Actually, that's the going rate for a soul in today's economy."

I laughed and took a drink of my latte. Joshua wasn't laughing.

"You're serious, aren't you?"

"Totally. Do you really know who I am, Adam?"

"Joshua Caine, trader in souls, collector of antiquities and rare books, with clients in the strangest places, and my friend."

"Yes, that about sums it up."

I thought for a moment, considered what I knew about Joshua, his talents, his apartment, and suddenly had a crazy thought.

"No, you've got to be kidding."

He started to smile and the sparkle was back.

"Okay, I admit, the 666 is a nice touch, and the books and paintings, especially Dorian Gray, would make me at least consider what you're saying plausible, but why would you make friends with me? Doesn't that go against who, or what, you are?"

"I guess that does present a problem."

"Adam, my name, and the mention of God, the Father, yes, they don't bring out the best in you. Your dress, your job, little hints here and there in your speech, and to have the collection you have, if it's real, you would have to be some kind of, of, I don't know—"

"Immortal?"

"Yeah, something like that."

He smiled and sipped his espresso.

"But the whole Joshua Caine name. You've got a play on the name Jesus and a synonym, or whatever you call it, of Cain, the first murderer. Why would you name yourself after Jesus?"

Suddenly, it made sense to me. The great deceiver, the father of all lies, the serpent, the clues, and words, and looks, and even his name made sense. I still couldn't believe it.

"I know you don't want to believe. That's okay. I'm not as hung up on faith as my friends up there." He pointed skyward. "I've created a real dilemma though."

"What dilemma is that? You might get into trouble for being my friend? What harm could that do? Aren't you already in enough trouble with your friends, sorry, ex-friends?"

Joshua laughed.

"I guess you're right. It's just that, I kind of like having a friend. A real friend, I mean. Someone who does things for me without expecting anything in return, and someone I can do nice things for without trying to lie to them, or deceive them, or get their soul. I just don't think my Father is going to be too happy about it, which I guess is a good thing."

"Good thing? Making God upset—" I stopped myself. Joshua was smiling.

"Yeah," I said, "I guess that's what you do."

"Yes, but I'm setting a terrible example for my angels. If word gets out that I've made a friend of a mortal than everyone is bound to do it. Do you remember what happened the last time some of my underlings made friends? Sons of God, daughters of men, giants, and then the Flood."

"A fabulous storyline for a great movie."

Joshua smiled again.

"You know, the Omen was actually quite well done. The Exorcist though, and some of these recent films just don't do me justice."

I had to laugh out loud.

"I just can't believe you are a regular guy," I said.

We finished our coffee and walked back to our apartment building.

"Don't you think the 666 and living at the DeVille is just going a little too far?"

"Not at all. Don't you think we devils have a sense of humor and like to have as much fun as the next guy?"

"I never thought about it."

We parted and I didn't see much of Joshua for the next several weeks. The school year ended, and things would have continued, but something happened that would change things, actually, two things happened.

I was home visiting my mother for the summer. One of my old teachers had stopped by. She had become the principal of my high school and was actually hoping to recruit me to teach closer to home. My mother was ecstatic. I wasn't sure, but the pay was better, and I would be closer to my mom.

The second thing was Katie.

When I got back to the city the first person I needed to see was Joshua. I mentioned my job, the move.

"That is wonderful news, Adam. Your mother needs you closer to home, and from what I hear, that new girlfriend of yours, Katie, she would make a really good wife. She's a keeper"

I didn't ask what he knew about Katie, or anything else. I didn't want to know. I could see that Joshua was happy for me, not miserable or sad, but actually happy. I also detected a small amount of sadness. He would miss me.

"We'll have to keep in touch."

"Yes, but only as friends, Adam. I don't want you as a client."

I laughed. I still wasn't sure if I believed him. Down deep I knew, but I didn't want to know.

"I'll send you a postcard when I get moved in," I said. "Perhaps you can visit sometime?"

"Perhaps."

Several years passed. I sent postcards, but never heard back. I sometimes thought I might have hurt Joshua in leaving. One day my postcards started coming back marked: Occupant No Longer at This Address. I felt bad that I had lost contact with him. I felt bad that I had lost a friend.

Another year passed, I was married, and Katie and I were expecting our first child. I had gone back to graduate school and was teaching part-time at the local community college. It was near the end of the school year, May 2006, when a strange package arrived in the mail. I didn't recognize the handwriting, but when I opened the box and read the enclosed card I knew exactly who had sent it.

My dearest friend Adam,

First, I must apologize for not keeping in touch, or for responding to your many postcards. As you probably know, I'm no longer at the DeVille. Without you there, life was rather dull. One day I just picked up and moved to a nice seaside condo in the East. Yes, as you can tell from the return address, I'm in Thailand, and I had nothing to do with the tsunami. I would appreciate a postcard from time to time, and I hope to be a better correspondent in the future.

I understand you and your wife are expecting your first child. I know I will not be able to be there, but wanted to send you a little something as a token of my happiness for you both, and as a token of our friendship. Yes, it's a U.S. Savings Bond, but I've also included an item I think you will really enjoy.

It was signed J.C. Irony and satire to the end

I missed my friend.

The U.S. Saving Bond attached to the note was in the amount of $10,000.

Beneath the card was a wrapped parcel. I opened it and found a first edition of C.S. Lewis's *Screwtape Letters*: it was signed by the author on the title page and accompanied by another card.

Clive had it right, Adam. He was on to me. He was a great writer, and a good friend.

J.C.

"Who is J.C.?" my wife asked.

"Jesus Christ."

I smiled, knowing that Joshua Caine was cringing and laughing at the same time.

THE RESCUE

HER COMPLEXION REMINDED ME OF THE SMOKED MEATS SERVED AT breakfast and when she spoke a nauseating cloud of cat urine floated between us. I thought of several cheeses I would rather not eat and genetics. My eyes returned to my wife and I wondered if the old adage about mothers and daughters was true. I shuttered and returned to the lunch buffet.

We had somehow found ourselves on a cruise with mother-in-law in tow. It all happened so fast, I can't remember if it was her doing or if my wife just failed to mention it. We were to begin on a river cruise starting at Kiev and navigating the Dnieper to the Black Sea and Odessa. The Black Sea and caviar will always be synonymous with my mother-in-law's dentures and when, unknowingly, I had approached the point of no return with little chance of going back.

The luncheon edged me closer to that point, reminded me of all the years of Maude chewing open-mouthed, flecks of food and spittle misting a shroud of filth over every blouse and t-shirt she owned. It was disgusting and even worthy of death, but the denture-clacking announcement that she would be moving in with us after the cruise—

"We're going to be late for the tour bus."

I jumped. I felt the urge to react in a mushroom cloud of sarcasm: I only had mordant venom for this woman. How my wife and I had agreed to accompany her for two weeks, as I said, is open to debate, but I am quite confident I had little if any input into the decision. I found myself in the middle of a geriatric cruise ship Mecca, a paradise for nostalgia and prescriptions. If the conversation, the navigation around walkers and wheel-chairs, the eating habits were not enough, there was the smell. No amount of river water or sea spray could erase the smell of age. If I was to put a color to it, it would be somewhere between a dehydrated yellow and a constipated brown. It was as if their clothing came pre-made with a scratch-n-sniff secret eau de toilette to offend the olfactory organs of those under the age of sixty.

"I'm sure we won't be late," my wife said.

"We will if Gordo makes one more trip to the buffet."

My name is Gordon, but Maude thinks it's funny to call me Gordo – *fat* – I had never really bothered to let it bother me, but now, I had been pushed over the edge with her announcement, her declaration of cohabitating with us, and had fallen down into the gutter of vengeance, revenge, hatred; something had changed in me, an alteration in my DNA, or some strange release of an adrenaline impersonator spreading the Seven Deadly Sins through my system. I wished I could blame my blood, but I couldn't: I had slipped into the realm of madness that only has one end: murder.

I realized I was well into executing a long overdue desire, something I had thought about frequently, and even written a few notes on for a novel I had been working on, but never had the fiction I wrote for a living turned to reality. I had to question if this was an anomaly, an innocent, unnoticed and unsolicited change in who I was. I also had to decide who was more deserving of death: my mother-in-law, for obvious reasons, or my wife, who I was finding more and more culpable in this whole cruise/move-in affair.

I had decided to liquidate my mother-in-law before we disembarked, yes, but now I was considering cashing in my wife's chips as well.

I knew it, had already seen it, had done it, and felt guilty about it, then forgot it a hundred times. Now, it was worse. Now, I pictured my wife, my wife changing, but instead of Jekyll to Hyde it would be daughter to mother, beauty to beast. What sleeping terror lurked that would drive sleep from my nights and peace from my days was subtler, deeper, darker. Internally, I had seen where my life was going, what the outcome would be if I remained as I was, a sub-conscious re-run of a movie already watched too many times. In that moment on the Black Sea, I knew it. It frightened me. It was inevitable.

I had to kill my wife too…

Then I thought of our son…

I don't have many fears. Terror, horror, I am prepared; I control my own Destiny, Fate only intervening at times making me powerless or unable to influence some outcomes. When I think of my son, handicapped, needing care for the duration of his life on earth, tears well up in my eyes, the shutter of emotion, like a child shivers in sleep after crying, and I am afraid.

I can't understand, can't get inside his head and comprehend him, or he me. It is frustrating, sometimes frightening, not knowing what is wrong, what he is seeing or feeling, or if I am the cause of his suffering, an effect, unable to solve or resolve.

The dreams, the fear, all were real enough, and that helped with my decision. I was determined. The hag, the horrible conniving interfering wretch was going for an extended swim. My wife would suffer, but she would be better off, we would all be better off.

Pushing the old bag off the ship I had thought would be easy. The propeller wash, the ship's engines, all would mask her screams, the late hour hiding any wisp of her falling body. All so quick, so sudden, I would not be missed, an alibi unnecessary, and I could work things out with my wife later. Kate would weather the storm and would not become her mother if I had anything to do with it.

"Gordon, are you feeling okay?"

Kate's voice startled me, and then I felt caught, guilty, but her eyes did not register what was in my mind.

"Just thinking," I said.

"I'm a little worried about my mother."

Her mother? Why should she be worried? Her mother just finished the first leg of a once in a lifetime cruise and was about to start on the second leg into the Mediterranean. And then, she would be moving out of the crap hole she lived in and moving in with us, probably be waited on hand and foot, the Queen of Freeloading.

"Really, why?"

"I don't know. Just a feeling."

Maybe her mother was finally realizing what a despicable and disgusting person she was.

"I'll try to be kinder."

I lied.

I would try to just stay out of her field of vision. Once we were in the Med, away from shore, off the stern she would go: goodbye, hasta la vista, sayonara.

The next few days surprised me. It was as if the witch was helping me set up her own murder. She would take walks late in the evening around the ship, always ending up looking out over the wake of the ship, watching the vast, dark sea. All I would have to do is sneak up on her and help her over the railing. It was perfect.

The night of the deed arrived. My wife was asleep. I had given her a sedative. She would be none the wiser and think I had been sleeping next to her the whole evening. I left our room and stole to the stern. Maude was there, but then something happened I had not considered.

"I know what you're thinking Gordo."

I froze. How could she know I was here?

"And you're probably right. So, why don't we just make this easy on both of us?"

Before I could move or even speak, Maude jumped over the railing and into the sea.

I couldn't move, my mind a blank, and then a thought drummed in my head, soft at first, and then loud and painful. Kate would think I killed her mother: cold-blooded, pre-meditated murder. Even if she had jumped of her own free will, what was in my heart made me guilty. If Kate found out – I could never tell her the truth. What if my mother-in-law survived?

I rushed to the railing, looked down at the wake: no sign of her.

My mind covered everything it contained and then focused on one thing: fear that my wife would become her mother. It went against everything I believed. People had the power to change, to control their Destiny, to be whatever they wanted to be. Why had I considered it, or considered killing Maude?

I had only one option, one choice, and I made it without thinking.

I jumped.

The water wasn't like concrete when I hit, not like dry concrete anyway – the chop of the propeller blades at least provided a cushion of air bubbles. I had grabbed a life jacket and a flotation device before I had leapt – falling overboard had been an accident.

The ocean was big… and deep.

I loved my son. I loved my wife. What had I done?

The wake stilled, but the ocean, big and bad and omnipotent rolled. It was a smiling roll, a chuckle, saying, "I have a few minutes to empathize with you, but then I'm going to kill you."

I scanned the undulating horizon. Nothing.

What had she been wearing? Polyester. Stink. But what color?

I looked for any sign of her hoary head, but only the ebb and flow of Poseidon's black beard between earth and sky looked back. The life vest didn't fit right, the arm holes too large, the shoulders battering back and forth against my head. The lifesaver, the round flotation device, already was numbing my fingers. I spoke out loud just to experience no one listening.

The water a whisper through my legs like an incontinent woman without a water closet or Woolite, up and down, a long car ride in summer heat between rest stops, windows down, hot breath of asphalt blowing everywhere but where the skin and sweat and urine congeal into a permanent stain in the underwear your mother advised you to change every day. The wet heat, soggy leprosy spreading, eyes stinging and nostrils shutting down in a dehydrated landscape with more water than a horde of thirsty whales could drink alone, the expanse, a life-giver and a watery grave, and for a moment, rescue forgotten, the razor sharp slice of rushing headlong into the churning form of the ship's excrement, a bubbly white line of peroxide-soaked purgatory and bleached Death, churning and boiling and breathing and wheezing and then the dark terror of loss, hopelessness, and regret. No time to reflect on a life well-lived or poorly-planned, no one and everyone to blame, and again, regret, a third-time, regret, but no rising from the tomb, no third day, no nail-marks or wounds, only a lone, leftover human soul soon to meet the consequences of a lifetime of poor choices, denial, and blame.

If I felt pathetic, my mother-in-law – my mother-in-law.

I blinked, watched the ship's silhouette merge with the stars, and then start to swim back to where she fell...

I thought of Dr. Seuss – One Fish, Two Fish, Black Fish, Dead Fish – when would the sharks come?

The vast table cloth of life spread out before me with its plates and flatware, the normalcy, the day-to-day routines, and with it the crumbs and stains along the way, the sweating stains of bottles and glasses in circles, the grease of a dropped pat of butter, and even the scent of age at the cloth's frayed edges. My mother-in-law had only been a single place-setting, a single item at a buffet that I could take or leave. I avoided her, never really tasted the experience, and had been prejudiced by her texture and aroma. Like a child's first impression, I shrunk away from the broccoli, or forced down the Brussel sprouts in the safe, secure promise that dessert would follow if I just cleaned my plate.

The salt in my eyes, in my mouth, and the tug of the lifesaver-shaped foam, the rub of the life vest and the friction of water reminded me I was alive. Maude would have nothing to buoy her up, nothing to give her hope, and perhaps her whole life was a desperate attempt to grab on to a line, a raft, a seat cushion, anything to keep her from sinking below the waves of insignificance, swallowing and choking and drowning in a life without love, without love returned, only lonely and alone surrounded by unnamable monsters and dark bottomless depths of black, black, black…

I laughed. I had called my mother-in-law Maude. A name, nothing really, but it gave her existence, a place, a spot in my heart. I kept swimming, searching, repenting…

Twilight breaking, I thought I saw her with the white caps, the familiar yellow polyester pants – Maude had created a flotation device worthy of an Eagle Scout. She saw me, unbelieving, drunk on desperation.

"Maude!"

I could see her blink, stutter in disbelief, and then a hope I had never seen before washed over her face. She struggled for words, spoke, barely audible.

"I knew you would come."

THE STRANGER WITHIN

The screams, loud and clear, and then quiet; something grinds metal against rusty metal: it stops and starts again. A smell, bone, flesh, hair, blood: greasy bile climbs his throat and clings to the back of his tongue. His head and hands tickle leaving him dizzy. A taste in his mouth: copper.

He swallows, forcing the burning liquid down with his fear, and increases his pace. He can see it now, the old chicken coop, his father's work shed. The squeak of the metal dies, almost whispers, like the last stale air leaving an unused room after the windows have been thrown open. An image of his mother flashes and then the door, hanging half open, the wood slats covering the old chicken wire.

His mother had kept chickens when she was still alive, when they were trying to survive, before his father had…

He pushes the memories away. The shed is the only structure standing between the house and the dark forest. The forest runs into the mountains, the dark shadow of trees, their eyes open, accusing him. He should have never left his sister alone.

The shed door is ajar; a sickly yellow light waxes and wanes, mingles with the smell of burning kerosene, like the growing smear in his throat. He tastes the color of phlegm between his teeth, sticking to the back of his tongue, and tries to clear it. The door taunts him, he pauses, catches his breath; he is afraid of what is on the other side. It is his fault.

There are no sounds. The air is still, only his breathing, and then his heartbeat is deafening in his ears. A sharp pain in his chest, his heart or lungs trying to explode, or his guilt. He swallows again and enters.

The old man, his father, standing, blocking his view of the small, tight room; the subtle hiss of the kerosene lamp throws sound and shadows, framing the old man in the dark walls, roof, and floor of the structure. The old man holds tools; a black liquid drips from one, and mingles with the scent of sweat and fear rising from the gloomy filth of the floor. At the edge of his vision, between his father and the flame of the lamp, he sees his sister's shoes dangling at the end of the work bench. He notices his father's hands again. A drill is tranquil in one; a saw waits patiently in the other. The drill bit draws his attention. Tangled hair fills the grooves dripping sweat and blood into small, equidistant spots on the wood-planked squalor.

"Come out, Evelyn. You can't hide anymore."

His father's voice jars him. He moves closer into the tight room.

"Jack."

Jack freezes. His sister's voice? Strange, distant, a shadow; he grabs for something, anything, a wood handle, an axe, a sledge hammer, he doesn't know. It makes a damp thud on the form in front of him. Light spills into his eyes, painful alabaster bathing the room as his father's figure falls, flees from the picture, falls down to the fetid floor like a setting sun. He can see everything and nothing. He can't comprehend the vision. Tears scream from his eyes and throat.

They came out West after the war, Jack, Molly, and their parents. The mountains, the clean air, and the lack of people were the main reasons for the journey. They had meant to go all the way to California, but something about the loneliness of the desert, the Utah Territory, interrupted their plans. At least that's what his mother had told him. His father's silence told the real story.

The old man had been on the losing side in the war. A rebel, born and bred in Louisiana, Pa had been schooled as a surgeon in Virginia. He was one of the first to join the Confederate cause. Jack had vague memories of his father before the war. After it was over, after defeat, the memories did not match the man that returned.

Jack was never sure if it was the surrender or a trauma, many traumas; his mother would not answer his questions, his father couldn't, or wouldn't. He just needed a place to recover, recuperate; a place to forget. Forget what? Jack had asked. There was no answer spoken.

Memories were hard to come by, as Jack had only been a few years old when the war started. His sister arrived only a month or two after their father had left. Molly had no recollection of their father before the war, and after the first years in Richmond, quickly had no desire to get to know the stranger. Jack tried to match the fading images, the Christmas tree, the new dog, the happy home in Richmond, with the man, but something dead was filling his father's place. The presence the war cast back into their lives was a silent ghost, a specter that never met one's eyes or listened. He would sit and stare into some other world away from Jack, Molly, and their mother. The only time they ever knew their father was alive was in the darkness of night.

The old man shrieked in his sleep, mumbled, cried; he would wake himself from some unspoken nightmare, a memory, and then he would sob. Their mother's calming voice always followed, as did the weeks and months and years that ended only in a change of residence. His father did not change.

Whatever was wrong with the old man, the relocation to Utah had no effect, other than it just got worse for Jack and Molly. The closeness of their quarters turned the sounds into ear-piercing screams, and their mother whispers became audible, calming their father, bringing him awake and back to reality. Then they would talk, and what little Jack could decipher he wanted to forget. He would try to think of his real home in the South.

The trip from Richmond was an exchange: a recovering war-torn land in the former Confederacy for something worse in the unsettled West. The journey by train felt long, although Jack did remember seeing wagons and other means of transportation. The transcontinental railroad had been completed the previous year, but there was still a break at the Missouri River. The tracks ended at Omaha, a bridge under construction, but then more rails followed and the Rocky Mountains: nothing prepared him for his first day in the desert.

They exited the sublime mountains only to be greeted by a wide and barren land that sloped up into hills and scrub brush, and then the forest and sharp, rocky peaks of the Wasatch. It was nothing like Virginia or anywhere he had been or seen. Jack thought it was a mistake, a dream, a place one traveled to in the imagination; only the damned would live in a place like Utah. Molly fell in love with the cursed place at first sight. She had no good memories of Virginia.

The old house their mother secured was really a log cabin. It had four walls, a sturdy roof, and a dirt floor. She quickly got to cleaning and securing furniture, as well as tools and other things they would need to fix the place up. Jack assumed the local Mormon community had taken pity on her and her situation: two young children and a disabled war veteran for a husband. A few weeks later, they had livestock and seed for a garden. They would need to work this land to survive, his mother had told him. The trip, the house, Utah, had not had any effect on Jack's father. He was still a shadow that flickered in the light of day, and only helped when his mother could coax him from his stupor, which was seldom. He would sit most days in a borrowed rocking chair near the entrance to their home.

The people were strange and had their own beliefs about many things. None, however, had any connection to Jack, except hard work. His mother had taken odd jobs in the closest town to their homestead to save money for clothing and other household needs they couldn't grow or make by themselves, and the homestead fell mainly to Jack. His mother was educated, and a talented seamstress, which won her many admirers, despite her being a Gentile from another faith. She taught Jack and Molly how to plant and tend a garden, to milk a cow and churn butter, to slop pigs and feed chickens, and even the basics of plowing a field with a horse, in addition to reading, writing, and arithmetic. Jack remembered Molly's face when she discovered that her little barnyard friends hadn't wandered off, but were staring back at her from her plate as breakfast or dinner. It was 1870. Jack was thirteen then, Molly nine.

Jack's father, the old man, never completely left his dream world, and rarely spoke to anyone, but things imperceptibly changed. His wife convinced him, Jack never knew how, to use the education and skills he had as a doctor. There would be no battlefield surgeries in this place, and it might help with the nightmares. His heart was never much in it. He set up practice in the same nearby town where his wife had found work, but he was an outsider, and few patients ever found his door.

Jack believed this pleased his father, but never spoke of it. It was probably a distraction from his family and the dark world he lived in, in sleeping and waking hours. When he would return in the evening, most of the chores were done, and he would find the familiar rocking chair and melt into his nostalgia.

Jack and Molly could have benefited greatly from their father's knowledge and experience, but he seldom saw them, even when they stood before his eyes. He had a routine, walk to town, do nothing, walk home, sit in his chair, silently eat dinner when it was ready, and then return to his chair. When night closed in, their mother would rouse him, and they would go to bed. His father's nightmares had not abated; his crazed words clearer in the confines of the one-room cabin and they were changing: instead of sobbing, curses; in place of his mother's kind words, tears.

He asked his mother once, but she didn't say much. Then he noticed the bruises, the different shades of yellow and brown, blue and black, on her arms and legs. When they started to appear on her face, he confronted his father.

"Mind your own business, Jackson. This has nothing to do with you, unless you want some of it?"

"What changed you, father? What happened during the war?"

Jack regretted the words the minute they had left his mouth. His father stood, his eyes bulging and the blood rushing to his cheeks. He picked up the closest thing he could find to strike with, the poker for the fire, but as he raised it, suddenly, it dropped from his hand. The blood drained from his face and even the color of his eyes seemed to shrink and darken.

"The war... The damned..."

His father walked away without finishing the thought, but that night, things got worse. Jack jumped out of his bed at the height of his father's curses and tried to intervene.

"It's nothing, boy. Just a bad dream. Go back to bed."

"But we can't sleep with you speaking so loud."

It was a lie, his father was yelling his curses, but Jack didn't plan on infuriating him any further than he had to. He just had to get the old man to stop.

The nightly arguments got worse, and even his mother had reached the end of her patience. Several nights, she called him out on his lies and curses, and at least twice, she left their bed and slept with Molly. Their father would rarely get up in the morning, and the days he did, he seldom made it to town. Jack felt something, a premonition that there would be an end to all of this, and it wouldn't be a good end.

Several weeks later, Jack and Molly had gone fishing. When they returned, they found their mother in front of the house, lying at a strange angle. She was still. Jack cautioned his sister back. He approached. Bright red blood had gushed from the back of her head and seeped into the dusty soil.

"Go find father!"

Their father was nowhere to be found. Together, Jack and Molly managed to get their mother into the cabin and on her bed.

"I'll have to go to town and find Pa. Will you be okay?"

Molly started to speak, but then someone entered the cabin.

"What happened here?"

Jack felt his blood chill. It was their father, and the tone in his voice was not anything he had ever heard from the ghost. It sounded too happy.

"Mother has been killed!" said Molly.

"What? What are you talking about, girl?"

"She's dead."

Their father moved to his wife's motionless body. He sat on the bed, put fingers to her neck, and then examined the wound on her head.

"Jackson, take the girl into town. Find the sheriff."

Jack was stunned. It had to be a bad dream. Nausea tweaked his stomach and whatever he had eaten that morning was coming back up. He forced it down, but the dizziness from blood being rerouted followed.

"Did you hear me, boy? Take the girl and get the sheriff!"

Jack jumped, but something dark had been forming in his mind, something much worse than his spinning head and churning stomach. He took Molly's hand and started toward the door of the cabin, but his mind was elsewhere. He remembered the muffled words and cries of his mother and the terrifying shouts and curses of his father, certain words, threats, and then his brain skirted to another memory, an image. His mother stood before him, strong and beautiful. She had said something, something important.

Jack, if something were to happen to me, you need to take your sister and get away from your father. He's not well.

"He killed her," said Molly.

Jack blinked. The memories stirred in and out of oblivion.

"What? What did you say?"

They heard their father approaching. Jacked turned. The old man, his head hanging, no emotion registering on his face, stood close. He had heard Molly.

"I'm sorry about this. I don't know what happened, but your mother is dead. I guess it's just the two of us now."

Jack looked at his father, and then at his sister.

"Don't tell me you didn't know," said his father. "She's not one of us. She's someone else's whelp, fathered by some coward who stayed home during the war. She's not mine."

Jack didn't understand. Molly started crying.

"Oh, don't start that, girl. That's what your mother always did when things didn't go her way. You're going to be a sad reminder of Evelyn, a reminder that I don't' want or need."

"You killed her!"

Jack's eyes widened. His sister's face was serious. He looked from her angry tears back to his father. He stood closer, towering over them, the anger in his face mirroring what Jack had only witnessed once, and then it disappeared just as fast as it had appeared.

"Believe what you want."

The old man turned back toward their mother's body.

"You hated her," said Molly, "and you hated me!"

The old man stopped, turned, a cold loathing flashed in his eyes, and something almost audibly clicked into place in Jack's brain.

"Did you kill her, Pa?"

His father didn't answer. He blinked, shook his head as if to clear his thoughts, and then seemed to hear Jack's question from a long way away. The answer, a question, brought his eyes back to Jack.

"What do you think?"

It was true. His father had killed their mother. It might have been an accident, an argument, but his father's eyes disclosed what Jack was already starting to believe. The old man tried to mix the truth with a lie.

"It was an accident."

"Are you going to kill me too?" asked Molly.

Before the old man could respond, Molly rushed out of the house. Jack started after her.

"Let her go, son. She's just upset. She lost her mother. She'll be back when she gets hungry."

Jack didn't believe a word his father spoke, not that he had ever really spoken to him. He waited. He would go find Molly later. He examined the man. Could this be the same person he knew in Richmond? The eyes, variegated with charm and kindness, but the darkness, the loathing, was just below the surface.

"I guess we better get to burying her."

A few months passed. His father had returned to his long silences. He seldom talked, which was fine with Jack. Molly was still his sister, no matter what the old man had said. He remembered their mother being pregnant before the war, and there was something else, caught at the edge of his memory, something important. He tried to think it out, but it just wouldn't come loose. Then one evening when they were eating supper.

"Mother was pregnant before you went to war with your child, with Molly."

"How would you know that?"

"I remember, and I also remember you were home, you came home from the war for a day or two, but you were already changing. I know you loved us, once."

Jack couldn't believe the memory had returned, or that he had voiced it out loud. He prepared for a curse or a blow, but neither came. He watched his father. The same, crazy glaze that had coated his eyes in their last confrontation was there. He was somewhere else. No amount of west desert air would ever cure his problem. Jack knew he had to leave; to take Molly and run away.

Jack continued to work the homestead, but he had a plan. In a week or two, it would be ready. He stowed supplies and other things that he and Molly would need when they left the old man behind. Molly, sensing Jack's plan, helped. She knew where their mother had hid her earnings, and she started to prepare their clothing. Maybe it was the sense of relief, the thought of leaving the old man behind, of escaping; whatever it was, Molly had found a fire inside her that wanted to burn their father.

Whenever their father mumbled anything, she would question him. If he had anything to say, she would contradict him. Jack could see whatever was still tied together in their father's brain start to unravel. His silence turned to curses, usually directed at Molly, and he actually was up and working. For some reason, the old man cleaned out the chicken coop and turned it into a work shed. Jack had no idea what work his father was doing, but at least it kept him away from Molly and their escape plan. The nightly arguments were easily ignored, until one night.

"Evelyn, you whore. You always had eyes for other men. I should have given you a beating sooner, then you wouldn't have strayed. We'd still be in Richmond if it wasn't for your wandering, and Jackson would still have a mother. I should have never left New Orleans."

Jack started. Was the old man seeing a ghost?

"I'm not Evelyn, and my mother never cheated on you, you old goat," said Molly. "I'm your daughter, and maybe you should have stayed in New Orleans."

Did their father really think Molly was his murdered wife?

"That's what you want me to believe, but I know it's you, Evelyn.

You've come back to haunt me. I knew you put the hoodoo on me, tricked me into marrying you, and now you've come back from the dead."

"Yes, I've come back from the grave because you murdered me."

"Molly!" said Jack. "Don't encourage him."

His father continued as if Molly was the only person in the room.

"Oh, I know it's you, Evelyn, all dressed up like a young tart. You can fool the boy, but you can't fool me. You've come back to torture me, but it won't work. I have a plan."

Jack put his hand on Molly's shoulder. She looked up into his face and bit her tongue.

"I know you're in there, Evelyn, and I'm going to get you out."

It was just the ravings of a crazy man, Jack told his sister later. He also warned her not to react to the nonsense and curses, to just ignore him. He also cautioned her never to be alone, especially with their father. Whatever his plan was, it could not be good. If he murdered their mother, he would murder them.

"You really think he has a plan? That he would hurt us?"

"I know he does," said Jack. "He thinks you're mother and..."

"You don't have to say it," said Molly.

A few days later, an incident drove Jack's warning home. Molly escaped with only a goose egg on her head and a bruised wrist. The old man had tried to cut her. Jack knew something worse would happen if they weren't careful, but what could they do? No one would believe them. He remembered Molly had gone into town once about their mother's death, but the people had already heard the news from their father. They thought the girl was just taking the news hard, probably due to whatever lies their father had spread.

Jack reflected. If they could just make it a few more days, the garden would be ready to harvest, and they could leave and start a new life somewhere else.

"A few more days..."

Jack closes his eyes and then opens them, the words still on his tongue. He looks over his father's still body, Death's gaze staring back at him. He turns to his sister, his eyes tracking the bloody footprints of his father around the workbench. The drill, that old drill, a tool from the war, from his surgery, and the saw. How many limbs had it chewed through? They were both still in his father's motionless hands.

He steps over his father's arm, goes to the work bench, reaches out; the sound of gears creaking and something falling to the floor. Molly is breathing; her fifteen-year-old hands tied together with rope, a new dress raises and falls with each breath, her brown eyes and freckles staring up at him. The vise left black marks on her temples. Jack looks at her, her golden brown hair, her motionless eyes, and the hole drilled in the center of her forehead.

"Jack?"

ERATO

Black ambrosia liquid inspiration
Buried in the dark
Dot to dots of the mind

The ellipses
Spider-webbing down down down
Deep into hidden teats that stalactite into
Dripping black icicles of sustenance

Ink and words
Stories beating bleeding
Bleating from the Muse's manila-thin lips
Leaving paper cuts on my heart
Why do I love thee so?

She whispers
Ringing silence in my ears
Tying my tongue and fingers tightly
Squeezing a drop of inspiration beading falling evaporating

Without warning
She ellipses into ink clots bulging
Breasts and hips and heat and sweat unrestrained
Birthing fluid stories in media res

Enchantress Sorceress Witch
Demon Lover
Tell
Don't show

Why I love thee so

FAMILLE DU JOUR

She had finally had enough. Divorce was something she had already forgotten. She would be only a memory when it finally hit him. This last meal would be perfect, and he wouldn't even see it coming. *I'm done*, she would say. *Goodbye.*

She wanted to blame herself for such a bad choice in a partner, but she could only bring herself to take the initial blame. What she had loved, no, been infatuated with, had turned out to be a spineless, introverted momma's boy. Why hadn't she seen that before they had taken their vows?

It started with his mother. She had to stick her nose into everything, and it didn't help that he told his mother everything. Every decision they made as a couple was actually made by his mother. She had complained. He had promised to grow a pair. The only pair had been mother-in-law and son. She had finally consigned herself to her fate. She still loved him.

That would have been enough for any woman to bear, but then came his siblings. The first was his brother, the entrepreneur. The only thing he succeeded in was finding the next pyramid scheme, the next bait and switch, the next opportunity to spend what little money she had managed to budget. That was when her love had turned.

Next, the sister, the conspiracy theory fundamentalist she called her when they were having a discussion. They never fought. He never fought. Every end-of-the-world fiction that had been posted on the Internet was filed in her sister-in-law's memory banks. Every survivalist tool, every end-of-the-world timeshare, every size and variety of food storage item had managed to eat up what little money they had left after multi-level-brother-in-law had taken his share. There was no logic, no common sense, no trust or intimacy: he would just follow his sister down whatever fanatical road she would lead him. She resented him, she hated them, she had come undone.

Finally, the holidays: every single holiday he had to get together with them, and she, being the good wife, had to tag along. It was pure torture to have all three of his living family members talking, all three of them cornering her, accusing her of not supporting him, blaming her for not doing enough to do the right thing, invest in the right scheme, believe the latest wacko. She thanked God her father-in-law had died before she had become a member of the family. She believed she would have died too if she had been the patriarch of such a brood.

It was Easter, and she had prepared their last meal. She would let him know it was over. The family would be coming over again, only this time things would be different. She had already severed ties, she had already cut communications, and she would serve them up, serve him up a large bowl of go to hell!

"I wonder what's taking everyone so long to show up," he said. "I hope they don't mind us starting without them."

"I'm sure they're just running a little late," she smiled.

They had started eating. The last dinner she would ever cook for him. This was the end.

"This is the best soup I think I have ever had."

"Thank you, dear. I worked on it all day."

Suddenly, her husband had a strange look on his face. He was chewing something. He reached his fingers into his mouth and pulled out something.

"What the? What is this?"

She smiled. She calmly got up and walked to his side of the table. She looked at what he held in his fingers. She said nothing.

"This looks like a fingernail," he said.

"Judging by the nail polish, I would say it belonged to your sister, dear."

She had always wondered what it would be like to cut a person's heart out with a spoon.

LOST AT SEA

The ice was breaking up. The change in pressure from the approaching storm had affected the frozen landscape. What had been a single mass of ice passable by sledge was quickly turning into a hundred small islands cast adrift on the open sea. Then the rain began.

There were thirteen of us to start: twelve of us apprehensive of living through the next day, one blind with a rage that had only one possible ending. Now, we were all alone with no hope of returning to solid ground. Our leader was still intent on pursuit of what eluded his grasp. He stood screaming at the approaching night sky and at his lost quarry. The sign had been fresh, we had been gaining on the thing that had slipped through his fingers, but now all was lost. My comrades and I huddled together on the broken ice to stay warm, spent from the chase of something we would never catch.

Day two brought the light, but no sun, and no heat. The fog that surrounded us muffled all sound outside of our own breathing, our heartbeats, and the steady lap of the sea's tongue consuming our frozen island. We had little food, and even less fresh water. Most of us would not consider the alternatives until Death started to visit each night.

Five days and five nights had passed with only the sea and the fog as our companions. The cold hand of Death that had been feared was now embraced: His icy fingers, now warm, had mercifully taken three of us during the fourth night, and more of us were soon to join our comrades in that endless sleep. The Night wrapped her frigid blanket around us for the sixth time in as many days, and only six would remain when she left us in the dawn of the seventh day.

The determination in our leader had not waned. What cursed thing had spawned such a burning evil in his soul, had kept him alive in the freezing nights and stolid days, no one could tell. Only great trauma to the heart could birth something so black in any living creature, and what remained in the cracks and crevices of that shattered organ was unnatural. It kept him alive. The water was gone, the food was gone, and we had nothing left but our dead companions.

What day, I could no longer remember. My life was ebbing away like our island of ice. I awoke to find only the two of us left alive. Why I continued to live, I do not know, but the man I had attached myself to was cursed to live, cursed as the Ancient Mariner. What ran in his veins was not the blood of man or beast, but the black fluid of unconscionable revenge. It blocked the pains of hunger and masked the throes of thirst. Today, I was certain, would be my last. I fell into a stupor, a gray realm between life and death, and felt the warm hand of Death touch my heart.

Time had ceased to exist. Had it been two weeks, or just two more hours. Only the dark cold shrinking emptiness of my stomach, the frozen dryness of thirst on my tongue, and the man were my only companions. Something had roused me, something that would keep Death at bay for a little longer. It was a smell, a coppery smell mingled with sweat and death. The man who had led us to certain destruction had finally given in, the heat in his shattered heart, the immortality in his black blood, had succumbed to the mortal weakness of the flesh. He carved a meal from the remains of my friends, my companions, and filled his belly.

There was an evil in his eye, no a madness, and it was also in the way he handled the knife. He expertly removed what little meat remained on the bones of our comrades. He saw me starring at him. For a moment he was caught in an unholy act, a flash of remorse may have even crossed his eyes, and then he just laughed.

"They're dead, aren't they? Dead and gone. What would they have done?" he said.

He threw a chunk of the frozen flesh at me. I was too weak to stand, and the very thought repulsed me, but the smell on this sanitized sheet of ice would not let me die. I crawled to the severed flesh and chewed.

Chewing the strip of frozen gristle brought some warmth back into my body. As the meat melted on my tongue the frozen blood reminded me of my thirst. He threw me another piece and I felt my life, not returning, but stirring somewhere in the core of my bones. I was guilty of an unpardonable crime, but I was alive. What punishment would God wreck on my soul, I did not know, but my heart beat and my breath came.

The remains of our companions were picked clean and discarded over the side of our dwindling refuge on the sea. There was nothing left, yet we lived. The evidence of our unholy deed melted with the ice, but my troubled conscience, and the thought that, very soon, one of us would be licking the bones of the other only added to the weight on my soul. Optimism had left me only wishing for the warm hands, the silent smile, and the kiss of Death. The man was obviously stronger-willed than I, and soon I would be a memory cast into the sea with the bones of my companions.

What day, I do not know, but a ship appeared. Was it God or the Devil who rescued us, rescued our temporal bodies, but left our souls tainted with the deeds we had done to survive? My master refused to board the ship if they hindered him in his quest.

There were questions from our saviors, a curiosity that would not be satiated; rescue and restoration of life was accompanied by a promise to aid and continue northward in search of what was now lost. The crew quickly feared my companion; they sensed the evil that he carried. In days they would regret their rescue.

The man, my master, was strong, but his body was not. Only his spirit hinted at recovery, but this was not to be the case. His rage was powerful; his determination never changing course, but his body was too weak to finish what he had started, what he had created. He was waning as the encroaching ice gathered around our vessel. The cold hindered our progress north; the sea had become a hand of ice stroking the ship with its frost-bitten fingers. I prayed for peace, and an end to this quest.

What divine or supernatural power heard my prayer, I do not know, but the ice closed in around us and locked the crew and the vessel into the middle of the frozen sea suspending all of our souls in time and motion. The ship would go no further. My master was at his end.

He must have felt something stir inside the remains of his heart: a confession or possibly a memory of life. In the dying embers of his rage he had empathy for the crew that had saved him from the sea. He began the long tale of what brought him to this lost ship in the middle of the north seas, and warned the captain to not make the same mistake as he.

I sat by his side as he narrated his life's tale, a story that withered on the vine of remorse and regret. I, his only companion, could not speak peace to his soul. He knew his time was short.

He had created his own troubles and had committed a great sin, and despite his moment of sanity he quickly turned to the darkness of defeat. He begged me, the captain, and the very crew that had plucked us from the sea to continue on, and to finish what he could not. I had no intention of following his mad dream, and prayed to any god that would hear me to stop this man in poisoning my new companions.

Several days passed and my master grew weaker. The storm that had polluted his mind and heart soon dispersed and released his broken and tortured body and soul. He was no more and his desire extinguished with him. Then it came.

I could sense it, even smell it. The thing that had fueled his hatred, the very monster that had been our quarry, had come to the ship. It had crossed the frozen sea intent on seeking the master. Whether it came to destroy or be destroyed, to repent or commit additional sin, I could not tell. It wept at the side of my master, his master, too late for reconciliation, or whatever its purpose was. It promised to join its maker in a pyre, in a tomb that knows no sound.

One of the crew, the captain, confronted the creature before it could depart. It was a dark, sad confrontation. The bane of my master's existence renewed its vow; it would disappear on the frozen ice and vanish from this mortal plane. It was over.

When the ice began to break, and the ship was free, they buried my master at sea. I am all that remains, and I alone carry the burden, the weight of guilt and sorrow, for my own actions and those of the man who became my master.

The crew mocks me. They can only see salvation, a reprieve from the icy destination that would have been their demise. They call me by the name of the man, the leader, my master. "Victor," they say. "Come, Victor."

I have become the Dog of Frankenstein.

EXPENDABLE

"JIM."

She tasted the word. A memory that she couldn't erase tasted the same: old pennies in her mouth.

No one had coerced her. Then again, it wasn't a single decision. A series of choices and actions led her to it, and to what would follow. She ran a hand over her skin. The cost had been worth it.

"No more doubts," she said.

Her reflection stared back from the mirror.

What's done is done, it seemed to say.

The consequences engorged themselves, their weight becoming perceptible, sprouting from places that had not held a thought or regret since childhood. They strained to break from her brain, from her heart. She felt their dirty fingers pressing against the inside of her skin. It was uncomfortable. She tried to think of something else. Romano.

"That is another problem."

A dark shroud rolled over her mind. She almost doubted the choice she would have to make. Why was she reflecting on the past, on Jim? He had been expendable too...

Or had he?

"It's too late now."

And it may be too late for Romano.

She found herself entertaining uninvited thoughts. She needed a distraction, not a conscience, innocence instead of guilt. Her reflection agreed, smiling, the perfection of every curve clearing her conscience.

"This is why," she said to herself. "I didn't get here on doubt or indecision or regret."

The mirror agreed, but also reminded her of Jim.

Jim had given her the mirror on their first anniversary. They were poor. They were students. Jim had saved his nickels and dimes, skipped lunches, and even took a few odd jobs to get the money to surprise her. She had been speechless. And then she had cried.

The fingers pressing against her insides were still there, still trying to escape, but weaker against her reflection. She felt something in the corners of her eyes. Her nose tingled, struck by an unseen hand. She wouldn't cry now. She had given up that weakness. She spoke to the mirror.

"You better watch yourself or you'll be expendable too."

She turned away and faced a gift she had given herself. It was a much more elaborate and expensive mirror, and more logical. She wondered why she had kept Jim's mirror. Maybe to hark back to Jim's sacrifice. Or maybe to remind her she had a heart once.

The dressing mirror was really a series of three mirrors, the center glass stood over six feet in length. Two moveable mirrors attached to each side, ovals approximately five feet in diameter from top to bottom, three feet at their widest width. They telescoped so she could see her entire frame, front to back.

There's enough glass for even Narcissus.

She laughed. Jim would have said something like that.

"If you could see me now, Jimmy," she said to the empty room.

She twirled, the mirrors revealing every inch, every curve; every particle of her body was on display, even the imperfections. Jim never noticed her imperfections, but that was then. There were no flaws now.

She cleared her mind and stopped spinning, her gaze resting on her posterior.

"Not bad for a young 35."

Jim was always happy, even after six miscarriages and the news she would never carry a child to term. He had tried to make her happy, tried to see the positive. She missed Jim for that reason alone. She cleared her memories, her eyes refocusing on her derrière.

"Your favorite part, Jimmy."

The darkening skies provided a perfect backdrop to the image she gazed on in the mirrors. She had lamps placed to light all of her curves, to remove all shadows, and to reveal any faults. There were no defects, and even if there were, they would be erased in a couple hours. The setting sun filtered out any background distractions. All she could see was her own form against a black canvas.

For a moment, the naked body that stared back at her was a stranger. She blinked, wondering who or what was staring back at her. The look of satisfaction on the lips of the woman was her own, the countenance of confidence, also hers. She drank in the likeness and felt a flutter of anticipation, even arousal. Her skin tightened in a chill of pleasure. She smiled and turned to face the image full on. The flawless skin and hair, the perfect symmetry, she didn't want to leave, but just keep staring at the inviting eyes that stared back at her.

"Don't want to be Narcissus, right Jim?"

She walked to her dressing table and sat down. There were smaller mirrors here, but the same pleased eyes smoldered back at her. She smiled, her nose crinkling in a wanton desire. She let the image staring back touch her perfection. There was pleasure in its leer.

When she finished dressing, the dark cloud that had threatened had grown. Jim, a good memory for the most part, refused to leave. He had been naïve, immature, and blindly followed his faith. It had been her faith too.

"Like faith ever did anything for me."

She had believed. It had started out innocent enough. The women at the church had been welcoming, friendly, but then the subtle undercurrent of competition touched her, nudged her into the water, and then carried her downstream. She was in deep water before she knew it.

It became clear there were two classes of women at the church they attended: those who had children and those who did not. The two classes divided and sub-divided into tens if not hundreds of expectations that no woman could ever meet. The imaginary list of perfections read like a beauty pageant instruction manual or a recipe for Prozac. If one was childless, she had to be practically perfect in every way to fit in: a Mary Poppins with an hour glass figure. Despite the hierarchy, she soon learned the child-bearing Fertile Myrtles feared the sterile super models.

Alone, away from Jim and church, she began to notice a similar hierarchy in every aspect of her life. Work, school, everywhere a competition was in progress, a prize fight, a death match. She started to doubt her faith, then herself, and finally, her husband. She could see his longing for children, his attraction to women who could provide him with an heir. He never said as much, but the message was on his face, on his lips when they kissed hers, and in his touch: Jim became expendable.

She grabbed her purse and coat. It would be a short evening and she would be home before the clock struck twelve.

"The Witching Hour."

She laughed to herself. She did a quick double-check of her apartment and left, locking the door behind her.

She got into a cab. The ride would only take 15 minutes.

"Where to?" asked the cabbie.

She gave an address and returned to her memories.

Chrissie Christian. That's what the infertile and obese called the woman at the top of the child-rearing hierarchy. She discovered truth in that coven of insecurity and medication. Women, people in general, loved to put down and demean others to feel better about their own pathetic lives. *Why set the bar so low*, she had thought. After the sixth miscarriage and getting her tubes tied, she decided to set her own bar. She was approaching middle-age but looked like she had just passed puberty.

"Are you sure that's where you want to go? That's bad part of town, not really good for a lady."

The cabbie distracted her. She was a little surprised, even appreciative. This cabbie was concerned about her destination. Everything kept reminding her of Jim.

"I'm meeting someone, so I think I'll be safe."

The cabbie nodded, still not convinced, even if she was meeting someone.

"I hope he's a superhero."

She didn't reply. Romano was no superhero, in fact, Romano was a coward. She had been thinking a lot about the man. Tonight she would have to make a decision, but not right this second. Her thoughts drifted.

Why had she ever been in love? How could she stay in love when she wasn't a real woman with working parts? Jim could never understand how she felt. Love wasn't enough for her, and even for Jim. He didn't have to say as much. Her feelings eventually boiled to the surface and then scalded everything and everyone around her. She shook her head.

The street lights passed by as the cab went deeper into the city. Jim was gone. She would never see him again. She still loved him, or maybe she just loved the idea of Jim. The seed money his life insurance policy provided had set her on her current path. Maybe that's what she really loved. She would feel better in an hour or two.

Ten minutes passed. The cab slowed.

"Why don't you wait here until whoever you're meeting shows up? I've stopped the meter."

"Thank you," she said. "You are very kind."

The cabbie smiled and then turned back to his steering wheel. She looked out the window. It was just like Romano to keep her waiting. She looked out the other window. The streets were dark, nothing moved, a reflection from a lone street light picked up the reflection of liquid on the street. She doubted it was water.

"Is that the person you're meeting?"

She looked out the front window. Romano appeared in the gaze of the cab's headlights. Right on time: his time.

"Yes, thank you."

She passed a twenty and a five through the cabbie's window.

"Keep the change."

"Thank you. Thank you very—"

She slammed the door silencing his appreciation.

"Are you ready?" asked Romano.

"I was born ready," she said. "Take me there."

"As you wish."

She had made her decision about Romano.

Romano led her down the dark street and then turned on a side street. Something had changed the man. She could hear it in his voice, see it in his walk. They turned into a darker ally. The smell hit her like a wall of feces mixed with blood, urine, and rotting food. The air was thick enough to taste, a palpable flavor in the absence of light and sound. The tang of pennies returned.

"How close are we?"

"We are here."

Romano unlocked a padlock and then opened a door cankered with rust and graffiti. The hinges protested. She entered. Romano followed. He closed and locked the door behind them. The darkness was as thick as the stench that coated her tongue. She could hear the machine, and then a click. The small room lit up, her purpose bathed in the light of naked light bulbs reflecting their incandescence off a plastic curtain that surrounded her destination. An instant and cheap clean room: everything was in order.

"Well done."

Romano remained silent.

She parted the plastic drape and approached a portable tub. Motors hummed, doing their work, circulating and heating the fluid in the tub. She set her purse on a nearby chair and started to disrobe.

"You are not shy, Señora."

"Señorita." She paused. "Shy has nothing to do with it."

She turned, topless, and faced Romano. Her stare withered the man. Most men paled at her perfect breasts, usually because their blood was rushing to other places. Romano's blood wasn't rushing anywhere. She could see the fear in him, smell it. He had changed. He met her gaze briefly, impotently, his anxiety withering his courage and even his natural lust. His eyes fell quickly to the floor avoiding her bare beauty.

"This is business, Romano."

"Yes, Señorita."

Romano parted the plastic and walked back to the door. A chair waited for him to sit guard in. She turned her attention back to the equipment and finished undressing.

She eased herself into the warm liquid. It teemed with life and entered every pore of her flesh. She relaxed until the warmth was up to her neck. She took a breath and plunged beneath the living liquid. A minute passed before her face broke the crimson surface.

"You have done well, my friend."

Romano didn't reply.

The treatment would only take 20 minutes, but when 25 minutes had passed, she decided to spend another 5 clearing her mind for what would follow. She had time.

She had rinsed off in a portable shower. The water was cold, but nothing she hadn't experienced before. It tightened her skin and strangely aroused her. If Romano was more her type... She laughed.

"Señorita? Is everything okay?"

"Yes, just thinking. I'll be right there."

She was almost dressed. Romano still sat guard. Perhaps an hour had passed. She imagined a time and place where she wouldn't have to hide or employ men like Romano. She could leisurely enjoy herself alone.

"I have a new phone for you," she said.

"Yes."

She heard the plastic curtain part.

"Did you get the money?" she asked.

"Yes."

There was a rough edge in his voice, an old wound re-opened. She had suspected this in the man. She knew what it was, but asked anyway.

"What's wrong?"

"I don't think I'm going to be able to do this any longer."

She stopped what she was doing and stood straight, her back to the man.

"The money isn't enough?" she asked.

"No, it's not that."

"Is it too dangerous?"

She turned to face him.

"I just don't like it."

She laughed. "You're not serious."

Romano still avoided her eyes.

"It's not the money, and it's not the danger, so you must have developed a conscience."

"Yes."

"Let me make sure I understand. You don't have to do the actual work. You just have to deliver a product."

She finished buttoning her blouse. She wasn't sure if the dampness was from her recent shower or her rising temper. She calmed herself and spoke clearly.

"We have a deal. I deliver the bodies, you deliver the blood. I even let you harvest the organs in the process and keep all the profits. Have you lost your nerve?"

Romano finally looked at her, but he couldn't speak.

"Have you found a replacement?"

"What?"

"A replacement, someone to take over your tasks?"

"I… I didn't…"

"You didn't think? Are you that stupid? We have a deal, and if you aren't going to fulfill it, you better find someone who can."

Romano was confused. He probably thought his life was in danger. He needed to think harder.

"This business is like a machine. If a part malfunctions it needs to be replaced."

Nervousness removed whatever mask of bravery Romano had been wearing. He was still speechless.

"If you're going to quit, I would hope you would have the foresight and initiative to at least find a replacement."

"I can find someone, Señora, I mean Señorita Bathory. Give me a few days."

"Thank you."

She picked up her purse and started for the exit, her hand reaching inside. Romano unlocked the door as she drew even with him. Before he could open it a razor flashed cutting him from ear to ear. She stood back to avoid the pumping blood soiling her clothing or shoes. She watched it spray and then wither into a slow stream around the man and down the front of his shirt. Her lips parted.

"I hate to see blood go to waste, my friend, but your blood is passed its prime. You are not young, and you are certainly not a virgin. I made that mistake once with an ex-husband. That kind of blood isn't good for the skin."

Romano was dead before the words reached his ears.

She opened the door and stood in the alley. She had a phone out and was already speaking.

"Can you be here in five minutes?"

She paused watching her surroundings. Romano's body fluid did nothing to improve the smell.

"Yes, save the equipment and then burn it down, and burn Romano and the other bodies with it."

She paused, listening.

"Yes, he's dead. Yes, Ramirez in Belém, he has contacts in the surrounding countries and can deliver the goods through the usual supply routes. I've already invited him take Romano's place. Did you send a car?"

She paused, listening, and then continued.

"Yes, this evening was more than satisfactory. Ramirez has a much better crop to harvest from in Brazil, a harvest of girls that no one cares about, no one remembers, expendables."

She disconnected the call and threw the phone into a pile of decomposing cardboard. She looked back at Romano.

"Expendable, just like you, my friend."

She walked back to the main street.

A car was already waiting.

HORSEMEN

If it wasn't the sand fleas; it was the stink... That was why he left... that, and the peace treaty. The piers, the boats, the people: so many half-eaten fish on a refuse pile of carcasses swarming with feces-tainted flies whose appetites were never satiated: a memory. Now, he saw water and gray sand and foam formed of lapping waves. He licked his lips. At least salt was clean.

Salt and heat and sweat and ache: he had worked on many boats, and on many coasts, sometimes until he felt like a fish himself. Beach-combing followed, the smell of low tide, seaweed, seabirds, and kelp, all good reasons to move west, far from the sea, farther from her fragrance, the surf, the salt, and her voice.

She reminded him of others, men, women, even the beasts and the serpent, all in the past, a savor never lost, especially in the heart. The dead sea spread out before him and he could see the Levant like it was yesterday. Another dead sea, another fisherman, a face he would see again, but not any time soon.

Inland he trekked from the sea, riding and walking on the dry land. Soon, the cool mountain air mingled with pine, and even snow, as he crossed the Sierra Nevada heading west. The smells and sounds were gone, but not the toil and soiled clothing, the loss and pain, and never having enough to eat. He did not miss the stench of the ebb and flow, of the flotsam and the jetsam.

When he and his horse had exited the mountains, a monolithic basin taunted him. Its endless sage brush and repressive heat reminded him of the salt-sown fields of war, the perspiration of whores, the salinity of tears, and the last sweat of regret that comes just before death. He blinked his eyes, but the images stayed.

His horse nudged him. He had ridden the old sorrel from the sea, walked and rode during the accent and decent of the mountains, and then the basin and desert. Sometimes they rode with purpose, but mostly wandered on foot side by side. They had nowhere to go, other than away from the sea. He rubbed her muzzle and examined her red coat; she needed a good rub-down. The sweat on her sides mirrored the foam along the edge of the lake, fomenting the birth of shrimp and gnats, mocking the brackish shoreline: the lake could not kill everything.

"You don't want to drink this, old girl."

She had been with him a long time, so long he could not remember. She was his closest, maybe his only, friend.

He watched the shore of the cyclopean sea and all the nightmares of his whole life stared back at him from the life-sucking muck that was more firm than wet. The fisherman returned to his remembrance, the futility of his life, his mission, and the few followers that spent their lives in much the same way as he had done.

He shook his head and stretched. He felt aches, especially in his gut, and with it came a touch of hunger. The lake looked back at him, forcing him to think of the last time he satiated his appetite on fish and bread. He felt a spasm of nausea wash over him. Why was it always there with the fish and the salt? A past deluge or miracle might be the source, but knowing the source probably wouldn't help. It was part of who he was.

He had crossed this barren waste believing if there were any more fish they would have left their salty births behind, and he had been right. The trout had been fresh-water born, and the mountains were salt free. The briny shallows that stared back at him now had no fish, only white death. He felt it, and then the familiar tick.

It was an impulse, an unconscious twinge, not of pain, but of emotion, of fear. He looked over his shoulder automatically. He had forgotten the habit in the mountains, alone with the old red horse, that feeling, that sensation one thinks he has lost, like seeing a familiar face, the eyes, the nose, the mouth, all familiar like a dream, but forgotten. It was an unbridled worry, a false fear, nothing.

His mother had the same nervous malady, not with people, but with water. Water and stoves and cooking and bathing and locks, all endearing impulses buried deep in an unsettled unconscious mind. That had been a long time ago, before anything else mattered.

He looked again seeing nothing but a vast wasteland edging up to a dead sea. He returned his gaze to his horse; she whinnied and stomped a hoof as if they had waited long enough in this godforsaken place and should move on. He waited, his eyes wandering back to the foam and water, his mind's eye to his mother. He couldn't shake the feeling.

His mother had only ignored the impulse once, and she had paid a terrible price. She had not heeded a premonition, not looked over her shoulder, and it had been a mistake. Lightning had struck and it had changed both their lives forever.

It was a long time ago, so long ago the earth felt young. Why think about it, or his mother, both she and the past were gone. Still, she could have warned him, should have warned him, locked the door, and never let the visitors in. She had known what they were going to ask him to do, to be.

He lifted his gaze beyond the lake and cursed. It wasn't Luck, but Fate. He preferred the old ways of thinking, the Greeks, they had it right, or at least they had entertained adherents to their beliefs. The Three Sisters of Night had cursed him and his mother. Why did they prolong his suffering? He could see them, gathered around their spinning wheel, their sewing machine, their needlepoint, whatever, and they cackled, watching his life, mesmerized by the thread that held him to mortality, the shears poised, the scissors opening, so close to cutting what remained of the string of his life that a soft breath or a whisper could break it. End it. But they always refrained from the final snip.

"Today would be a good day to die," he said to the horse, "but if you drink that water you'll just wish you were dead."

He laughed. Were the three Fates really hags: they were probably beautiful women with a job to do, a task set before them, more like him than not. In another life, another world, he may have courted one of the Fates, proposed, even married her and, together, made a large family and died a happy man. He laughed again.

"Just a job, I guess. Maybe next time."

The horse shook its head, as if in understanding, and nudged him forward. It wanted to get to the next town and fresh water.

"And something to eat," he said absently.

Something moved; a glimpse of something where nothing had been before. It was a dot in the corner of his eye. He scanned the spot and everything in its vicinity; it had been in the lake, on the lake. He strained and barely made out signs of civilization in the distance beyond the lake's opposite shore. There was a city there, he had passed through it once before, but had forgotten its name. The movement had nothing to do with the city. He fixated on the spot. Nothing, he had imagined it, and then it was there again, just at the edge of his vision, something moving, coming across the lake. He squinted, tried to focus.

The endless salt flats had lulled him into complacency. Mirages were everywhere, the waves of heat or light displaying false shapes, ghosts, anything but reality. It had been troubling at first, but now he could tell an illusion when he saw it. This was no illusion. The sorrel stamped. She could see it too, sense it. She knew and he felt what she knew. The same thought had crossed his mind twice, but he had looked behind, not at what lie before them. The color would make it clear, confirm what he already knew.

It was dark, black, and it did not shimmer. It was no mirage. It moved slowly, but with purpose, coming across the deceased waters as if on an errand, as if some unknown power had willed it to move. There was no unknown power, only a cast of unfamiliar powers.

It was riding something, some animal, but not a horse. It had to be a horse. What else would a man ride, if it was a man, and what else could it be, but a man, or at least what had once been a man. How did he stay above the water? He had heard of water so salty that a body could not sink or even drown in it, but salty enough to ride on? This was no Jesus Christ or Peter, especially dressed in the color of night and riding a–

His hand went to his belt. The Colt was where it should be, the handle smooth and familiar from use. He had cleaned and checked it that morning. He went through the habitual procedure every morning, and every night before he went to sleep. He always had to be ready.

The figure continued to bear down on the spot where he and his horse stood, as if some magnetic power pulled it, an unseen hand pushed it, closer and closer. It was a figure now, shaped like a man, taller than most, and it was riding a horse, a pale horse that deepened to the black of midnight. The image had blended with the colors of sun and salt and water giving it a hue of silver, gloaming, and then full darkness.

He relaxed, but kept his eyes fixed on the pair, his fingers lightly on the butt of the gun. He moved next to his horse, a hand on her neck, and waited.

The rider and his mount hesitated. They still came forward, but there was a tension. He had not felt this kind of strain in a very long time – not fear or anticipation, but reluctance. He blinked once and refocused on the rider.

"I thought you might be coming this way. I see you've given up the sword for something a little more modern."

"Practical," he said.

He examined the familiar figure: dark boots, an oilskin coat, and a well-fitting ebony hat. It must have been burning on the inside of that getup, but did it matter? Blackie had always forsaken comfort, the *practical*, for style: it was all about the grand entrance, first impressions, and Blackie never disappointed.

"I thought only the destroyer rode upon the waters."

His eyes moved down the figure; there was nothing but smooth lines, as if the horse and rider were one. He was sure there were two gun-metal gray .45s with handles matching a starless night sky beneath the water-resistant duster, both probably tied down to the rider's legs. Blackie spoke again.

"You might as well keep going. You're wasting your time in this town. It isn't the right time. I've already tried."

He removed the bandana that had half-covered his face revealing a weathered countenance. He smiled, his teeth the color of his white skin. He dismounted. His horse moved toward the sorrel, they nuzzled, renewed acquaintances, and ignored the two riders.

"That was a nice piece of work you did in '49. Gold Rush, indeed. Kind of an enjoyable follow-up to the Treaty of Guadalupe Hidalgo," said Blackie. "Sorry to hear about that. It didn't quite work out, did it?"

"You get around."

"I keep my ears open. I hear there's some real trouble brewing, probably in the next year or so, '58 or '59, maybe later."

Blackie clapped a hand on his shoulder. It was friendly, but the touch reminded him that he was hungry. He felt his stomach twist and then complain, empty.

"My money's on Richmond," said Blackie, "but these people here seem to think one of the Carolinas is where it will start. Can't remember which one."

"I believe the *thus saith the Lord* goes something like *wars that will shortly come to pass, beginning at the rebellion of South Carolina, which will eventually terminate in the death and misery of many souls.*"

"Yeah, that's it," said Blackie. "I never was much for remembering scripture, Red. At least you were mentioned in this one."

"And Azzy," he said.

"Yeah, that old owl hoot. Never did like his nickname."

Blackie laughed, but his face was uncomfortable. He mapped its surface, navigated the lines and curves and movements, but there was nothing there other than fear of the pale rider they called Azzy. He spoke.

"I had nothing to do with the Gold Rush, or Hidalgo, or anything else."

"Sure, whatever you say," said Blackie.

They looked at each other. There was a certain empathy in the dark rider's eyes, an understanding. He opened his mouth, but then closed it. He looked at the two horses.

"Been a long time since these two had a roll in the hay. Maybe we should travel together for a few days, let them have a little fun, catch up, you know. What do you say?"

He said nothing. He was tired, thirsty, and hungry, more so with the appearance of his old friend. He liked being alone, away from people, and away from friends. It was better, safer that way. He studied the path around the south side of the lake. As if reading his mind, Blackie spoke again.

"We could travel south. I hear there's a really nice place on the Old Spanish Trail, plenty of grazing, and no shorelines or fish or salt."

His gaze snapped back and he almost reacted, the words coming up his throat, stopping on his tongue, and then melting away with his saliva. His hand had already drawn his gun.

"Take it easy, I know how you feel about seas and fish, and especially salt. I just wanted you to like the place, that's all. Somewhere you don't have to think about the past."

"Or the future."

He relaxed and replaced the .45 in its holster.

"The future?" asked Blackie. "It's the past that bothers you."

Blackie frowned, a hand came to his chin, and then he smiled.

"Most of that was Azzy's doing anyway, and you have to admit, it made the stories much more interesting. Turned it from straight up, wrath of god non-fiction horror to fantasy fiction, maybe even fan fantasy fiction."

He nodded. He still felt tension, anger building up within him, but he pushed it aside. Azzy's doing, yes, and what could Azrael have done differently? Not much any of them could do differently, nothing they could change, the past, present or future; it was just one eternal round. They had all, each one of them individually, been called and set apart for a purpose.

He looked at his old companion and almost smiled.

"Non-fiction horror and fan fantasy fiction, huh? You're talking genre when they haven't even come up with the names yet. They still think it's the word of God."

"I don't know. Some of 'em are starting to think it might be fiction."

Blackie laughed again and continued.

"I mean really, a global deluge."

"Don't forget the plagues."

"Egypt, now that was a good time," said Blackie. "I was there for seven years."

"Yeah, I remember, and I remember what followed."

Blackie seemed lost in a pleasant recollection, a commemoration of better days. Neither spoke for several minutes. The wind started to pick up; he was thirsty and hungry. He had mounted his horse when Blackie spoke again.

"Moses wrote some pretty good fan fiction, didn't he?"

"Imagine the day when they come to the realization that all scripture has been so messed up by man that there's hardly any truth left."

Blackie shivered and went back to his horse. He mounted in one fluid motion.

It was sad, really. The truth was still there, but people had to look, had to really look.

He nodded toward the south.

"Old Spanish Trail on the way to California? I just came from there, and I don't intend on going back any time soon."

"We're only going to stop for a night or two, and not even go west. We let the horses get to know each other again, and then we can move on, move farther south," said Blackie. "I hear there's a really nice cantina in this new place along the Mexican border. Tombstone they call it."

"Tombstone, you sure?"

"Well, if it's not Tombstone, it will be in a few years," said Blackie.

"When Whitey and Azzy show up," he said.

Blackie stared at him, as if considering. Two more friends, a possible rendezvous, and–

"Funny, I forgot about your jovial side."

"You mean sarcasm," he said.

Blackie paused. "You may be right about Whitey and Azzy."

He watched his old companion and then pointed his horse forward around the south side of the lake. Blackie caught up and kept pace next to him.

"The weather will be better. You know how it gets here when summer ends. We can be to the trail by early September, and then down to Tucson before the snow really starts to fly," said Blackie. "That reminds me, weren't you down there in '21 with these folks?"

"No," he answered. "That was the Mormon Battalion and they captured Tucson without my help."

They continued in silence. The city was getting closer. Blackie turned to look behind them, and then in front. He finally spoke off-handedly.

"Who knows, maybe Whitey and Azzy will already be there."

"Like old times."

"Like old times." Blackie laughed. "Well, it's a heap better than this place. I really tried to do my thing, wind and rain, snow and ice, drought, I even brought in some black locusts in 1848, but somebody up there must like these people."

"Black locusts? Crickets?"

"Yeah, I thought it added a certain *je ne sais quoi*."

He shook his head and a smile started at the edge of his mouth. Despite everything that had happened over the years, he still liked Blackie the best. He had always envied the black clothing. He looked across the water; the city had grown, like the people that inhabited it.

"I heard you and the others have been riding with this group since 1820 and–"

"Now that's not true," interrupted Blackie. "I may have checked in on them a time or two over the years, but I haven't been riding with them. In fact, I ran into Whitey at Fort Bridger last year. He said he hasn't seen you or Azzy in years, except for that incident in 1844."

"Carthage, yeah, I remember."

He looked away. He felt the anger seethe again.

"So, what are they calling this place now? It was Deseret, right?"

Blackie did not answer.

"What? Is there something about the name–"

"Salt Lake City."

Blackie interrupted and spoke so quickly that he barely caught it. Salt again: instead of anger, he smiled.

"Now that is irony, isn't it?"

Blackie laughed. "I knew you would get in the spirit of things."

Maybe a few days wouldn't be that bad, and there really wasn't that much between this great salt lake and the Mexican border. What could happen? It was a wasteland with a few scattered settlements and a displaced Indian tribe or two.

"I need to get something to eat."

"A few days on the trail, we can talk about old times, and–"

"Does our destination also have salt in its name?" he interrupted

The man in black laughed.

"You're going to love it. Not that many people, plenty of grass for the horses, and–"

"What is it called?"

There was a familiar twinkle in Blackie's eyes that only made his black clothing blacker.

"Mountain Meadows."

AUTHOR'S NOTE: This story originally appeared in a collection focused on Utah horror. If you, Gentle Reader, are coming to it with no knowledge of Utah history, the ending may be a little unsatisfying. The Four Horsemen of the Apocalypse may be obvious, but Mountain Meadows may not. On September 11, 1857, local militiamen in southern Utah aided by American Indian allies massacred about 120 emigrants who were traveling by wagon to California in a highland valley called the Mountain Meadows. According to Richard E. Turley Jr., Managing Director, Family and Church History Department of the Church of Jesus Christ of Latter-day Saints (LDS), two particulars make the event difficult to explain. First, nothing that any of the emigrants did or said came close to justifying their deaths. Second, the large majority of perpetrators led decent, nonviolent lives before and after the massacre. For additional insights, see *Massacre at Mountain Meadows* authored by Turley and other Latter-day Saint historians, Ronald W. Walker and Glen M. Leonard (Oxford University Press, 2011). It might also not hurt to know a little LDS history, including Joseph Smith and Salt Lake City, to really get everything in the story.

SAFARI

"You not have anything like this in America I bet. You like it very much I think."

I already didn't like the man. I kept an open mind about the tour.

"China only place in world that has this. China number one."

His pride was as large as his humility was small, but that wasn't what bothered me. It was his smell. It reminded me of the first time I smelled my own stink. I think it was in the fifth grade. It was Ritz crackers, at first. Then it got stronger. The man spoke again in Chinese to my translator, Li Ming. His breath complimented his rancid animation.

When we arrived at the Safari Park, I was already suspicious. Why my hosts would put this on my itinerary was a mystery. Li Ming just smiled when I asked her about it. We stopped in front of a dilapidated building, a large fence spreading out to both sides like broken wings. I wondered if this was to keep the animals inside or curious people out. I followed Li Ming from the car and walked from the present back in time through fading paint and sub-standard architecture, rust, the smell of feces and rot, and Chairman Mao. It all reminded me of the irritating man and his eau de toilette.

Li Ming acted as if this was her first time at the Safari Park, but I saw a knowing look when her eyes met the man's. He had been in a lively discussion with several other ticket holders, who were likely joining me on the tour, when he saw us. I had a feeling he was my unofficial minder, part of the state secret police, something carried over from the Economic

War of the twenties. His presence put Li Ming on edge. I wasn't the only one being watched.

"You will like very much."

"I hope so," I said.

A bell sounded and then a harsh voice barked something in Chinese over the loud speaker. I looked at Li Ming.

"It is time for us to board the tour bus."

"Really? A bus?" I asked.

The two dozen or so people that had been milling around, all Chinese, formed up like well-trained soldiers in a line at the voice's command. They moved in an orderly fashion toward a door that probably led to the bus. I thought of a furnace: a mass execution. I followed Li Ming.

The door opened into an ancient garage. A vehicle from another time and place stood waiting, a time machine that would take us into an Africa that no longer existed. The smell of oil and gasoline, banned substances, as well as rubber and dirt hung in the room. I thought of my grandfather, a fossil fuel aficionado who maintained several combustion engine dinosaurs from the early 21st century until he died. His cars were in museums now. The man's voice vaporized my memory.

"This replica of bus station from 1999. Not real."

I nodded. His teeth the color of kippers flattered his breath. He moved to the front of the line and positioned himself at the doors of the bus. They opened. The others started to board, organized and patiently, each showing his or her ticket. I felt nostalgia, or perhaps irony; China had changed so very little in the last century. Some things would never change.

The man spoke to each rider, their reactions betraying his status and position. I was sure he was my minder, the breath and body odor must have been a disguise. As we approached for our turn to board, the man's face turned to an exaggerated smile.

"I save you good seat in middle. You see everything from there."

"Thank you."

I climbed the steps. A mechanical bus driver with a painted on face greeted us in Chinese.

"Welcome to Safari Park. Watch your step," Li Ming translated.

I turned down the narrow aisle, the worn vinyl seats period perfect. I jumped, my breath caught, and then I laughed. Something had caught my peripheral vision; a chicken, several chickens. A cage on the first seat behind the driver was full of them. I stepped past the cage, through another time warp, onto a real bus in a land far, far away. Instead of Spanish or an East European dialect, I heard Chinese. I continued back to the only empty bench seat left open. It was in the middle of the other smiling tourists.

My travel companions were all joking and happy. I wasn't sure if it was real or an act, part of fooling the foreigner. Li Ming sat down next to me. The man boarded and the bus doors swung shut. There was a sudden shaking accompanied by a loud noise. Everyone quieted. I thought I heard, or at least felt, a pre-2000, diesel-powered combustion engine and then I smelled exhaust. I was sure most of the people on the bus didn't even know what a combustion engine was, but they probably knew the smell of diesel. China was still the biggest offender of unauthorized and sanctioned fossil fuels use. Would the Chinese openly violate the Federation's ban? I remembered the bus driver. Safari Park apparently spared no expense in making the experience as realistic as possible.

I imagined an archaic computer system commanding the seats to vibrate as if it was a real bus. A program activated the sounds of a real engine, and apparently piped in the smell of burnt fuel. The garage door in front of us was opening in-sync with the program, the advertised African adventure greeting us like the rising sun. I wasn't in the mood. It would be as highly scripted as everything else in China had been on my trip. I looked out my window.

Westerners were becoming more common in China, but their visits were limited and watched, even in the larger, supposedly cosmopolitan, areas of Hong Kong and Shanghai. I wondered why I was the only foreigner on the bus. I had been with a group of journalists covering news in Beijing. The invitation for the safari had come and I had thought some of my comrades would have received the same. I asked Li Ming.

"Yes, several of your fellow journalists received invitations, but you were the only one who responded."

I wondered if this was true. My colleagues had all been to Beijing many times. This was my first visit. Perhaps they had already experienced Safari Park. I turned to watch the scenery. So far, we had seen the Communist era's finest concrete and rebar and their prohibitions against mouth and body hygiene. I wasn't looking forward to what would come next.

Despite China's embrace of the free market system in the late twentieth century and its willingness to join other countries in democratic reforms in the twenty first century, the country was much the same as it had appeared in print journalism a hundred years ago, including its prejudices and fears. A westerner was still an alien, a possible spy, and at worst, a journalist. I was the latter, my trip arranged and scripted in the hopes I would report to my western masters the progress China had made on several fronts, pollution and human rights leading the charge. I still wondered why I was on a cheap, zoo-themed ride. The irritating man was making his way back to me again.

"This not real, not fossil fuel engine, only simulation."

I nodded, as if the cheap imitation had fooled me. It was clear he didn't want any mistakes in what I would see or believe. He emphasized the Federation's mandate.

"We take great care protecting environment."

The bus lurched forward, the computerized driver's head spun around on his neck with his painted on smile, laughing and motionless saying something in Chinese. The people around me laughed. I looked at my translator.

"He says, sorry folks, I was out a little late last night."

The Chinese, despite their disdain for the West, were doing their best to appear as normal as the foreigners they entertained. The driver was painted up like a lush from America. I could only imagine his recorded voice would make him look like the part he was playing: a colonial idiot who had destroyed the real Africa and threated China all the way back to the Opium Wars.

"Have a nice tour."

The man interrupted the driver's speech file. He smiled at me and returned to his seat. I sat back, looked out the window, trying to get the image of his teeth out of my mind. I prepared to waste at least an hour.

The flora and fauna would have convinced any virtual user that they were really in Africa, any virtual user that accepted things as they appeared, that is. I could see most of the scenery was fake. The driver's head spun around, the programed tour narration continued. Li Ming translated.

"Please keep your hands and arms inside the bus at all times. Safari Park is not responsible for injuries sustained by individuals who do not follow the rules. There may be lions, tigers, and bears."

The bus moved a little faster. I sensed anticipation and a little anxiety in my safari companions. Despite progress, the Chinese still had a naïve trust in everything they heard from official Chinese sources, even if the source was a broken down robot driver selling them a bogus safari in

Africa. They also liked to believe in myths and fantasies, superstitions, and this tour bus ride was tailor-made for the Chinese imagination. My translator kept up with the occasional comments and narration. I listened with one ear and looked out the window as each manicured clump of plants or bull-dozed grassy knoll passed by.

My travel companions were attentive, as if sitting in a college class. They really believed they were in some exotic clime with lions and tigers and bears waiting around every bend. I wondered if the animals would be as real as the driver. The first thirty minutes of twists and turns was complimented by the pre-recorded script. Anticipation and even fear were swelling in the captive audience. I was falling asleep.

We traveled through a grove of trees, around man-made blind curves, and even through a chocolate brown river. The driver warned of piranha and crocodiles and my companions got close to the windows, careful not to open them, there communicators coming out to take pictures. I listened to Li Ming.

"There may be gorillas or pythons in the trees above. Be careful."

There were no animals in the trees above, or in the brown water, but that didn't stop my companions from taking more pictures. I asked Li Ming if we would see any real animals.

"I don't know. I've never been on one of these safaris."

I wasn't sure if she was telling the truth. I asked about the man that had spoken English to us. If he had been assigned to watch us.

"That is the old China," said Li Ming. "He's probably with the safari company, just showing off."

I believed Li Ming's last words. I sat back in my seat, resigned to my fate, and thought about my hotel bed. Li Ming sensed my ambivalence and my boredom.

"I am told there is a spot along the route with lions and tigers and you can feed them live food."

That explained the chickens and now I understood what the man meant. China had been the only country in the world for almost two centuries that allowed the feeding of live food to animals for entertainment purposes. I smiled and returned my gaze to the heavily manicured African jungle. This was more like ancient Rome than Africa. The trees were getting thicker, the light darker, and I expected the climax to appear at any moment. The last thing I wanted to see was a programed feeding of programmed wild animals.

Suddenly, as I had expected, the bus ground to a stop. It felt like a malfunction. I sat up and looked around. We were in a clearing, trees arching above us on one side, and a grassy field directly in front of my side of the bus. I scanned the area and blinked. I rubbed my eyes and looked again. A lion, no two, three, four lions were coming across the clearing to greet us. The man had stood up and was saying something. His words were sardines on crackers.

"He says that if anyone is brave enough, and has 5 credits, they can feed the lions."

The man continued to talk, reaching into the wire cage and withdrawing an unsuspecting chicken. He waved it around, taunting the crowded bus. I was sure he was demeaning them, questioning their courage, all in an effort to earn some extra money. This was inhumane and condescending, not only to the people, but also to the lions, and especially to the chickens. I had had enough.

I wished I was anywhere but on this bus. I watched the man for the lack of anything else to do. He moved to the side of the bus and slid the window open. I could feel mass panic rush through the crowd. I smiled. No lion would fit through one of these windows. I was tempted to open my own.

The man held the chicken out the window, waving it, the lions converging on the spot just below the chicken. One of the lions leapt up, but the man anticipated it. He pulled the chicken back in, taunting the big cats. Li Ming was right. This guy was a show off.

The show went on for several minutes. I was disgusted. The man's mock bravery, the chicken's fate, the lions, and the captive audience; what bothered me most was what they had done to the lions.

Once considered the king of beasts, these lions looked like overgrown cats that probably couldn't catch their own meal if their lives depended on it. Their fur was matted and looked slept in. They had been conditioned to eat when the bus approached, instead of a bell the sound of a fake diesel-powered engine. This was probably the only meal they had each day. I felt sorry for them. Then the man spoke in English.

"You brave American. You have money. You feed lions."

The man was walking back to me, chicken in hand. He was saying something in Chinese and then made the sound of guns. I didn't need Li Ming to tell me he was mocking America's old Wild West.

"You feed lions. I give you this one on house."

I shook my head. "No, I don't think so."

"Why, you afraid? You think it bad? You think chicken should have rights like humans?"

He spoke in Chinese again and the bus laughed, but it was a nervous laugh.

"Tell them I don't find feeding chickens to lions very entertaining."

Li Ming looked at me as if she couldn't understand my words. I repeated them.

"I can't say that. It would be offensive."

"And what he said to me, what he's been saying to all of these people, that isn't offensive?" I asked.

Li Ming didn't respond. I could see she knew I was right, but she was afraid, afraid to get into trouble, or maybe lose face.

"It okay. You woman," the man interrupted. "Woman not brave in America like Buffalo Bill or G.I. Joe."

I smelled yellow. I hated this man. I wanted to stand up and slap him silly. I wanted to feed him to the lions. I turned away, bridled my emotions, and looked out the window. The lions were still there, waiting for their handout from the welfare state. The man went back to the open window and started teasing them again. A story was forming, but I needed a good ending.

Something bumped the bus. I couldn't tell what or where, but it felt like another vehicle had hit us. The bus rocked and then was still. A second thump, on the roof, and the bus rocked some more. I listened. Padded feet walked along the roof, claws taping the bus's metallic skin. The bus grew quiet, even the irritating man and the chicken were still. Fear of the unknown was playing with the group's emotions. I sat back, another gimmick, and then the screaming started.

The man, who had been so proud and brave waving the chicken out the window, was pressed against it, his shoulder forced out the opening, his neck at an odd angle. The sounds on top of the bus had distracted him too. He left the chicken, his hand and arm attached, dangling out of the window, outside the safety of the bus. The man's hand, wrapped around the chicken's neck, was wrapped inside a lion's mouth, the lion's weight pulling the man against the window.

Everyone started screaming and moving away from the man and the open window.

"We need to help him," I said.

"We can't get to him," said Li Ming.

She was right. The rest of the passengers blocked our way out of our seat. I watched in horror as the man screamed in pain and the tourists moved to the back of the bus. Then, without warning, a second lion jumped to the window, its snout pushing the man back inside an inch, maybe less, jaws open and then closing on the man's neck. The lion's paws pressed against the closed windows that bordered the open one, and then the man was gone.

A vacuum sucked him from the bus into cold and airless outer space, but instead of frigid blackness and a quick death, the lions converged on the man. They no longer knew how to kill, only how to eat. I felt sick, wanting it to end.

The man's screams rose above those on the bus. I couldn't believe he was still alive or able to scream. The mechanical driver's head spun, spouting something, followed by a laugh.

"What did he say?"

I tried to get Li Ming's attention, but her eyes were locked in terror on the man and the lions. Everyone watched in horror.

"Li Ming, what did the bus driver say?" I repeated.

She looked at me as if I was speaking a foreign language. I grabbed her shoulders and repeated what I had said again.

"It is making fun of us, telling us not to be cowards or cheapskates, and to feed the lions."

For a split second I thought this was part of the script, a bad horror story, but then I realized the man was never on the menu. The bus driver's program mirrored the man's disparaging remarks. It heckled the tourists into buying chickens, not to join the irritating man on the lions' lunch menu.

The bus rocked again. Were more lions falling from the trees? I turned to see a lion drop from the top of the bus to join its companions in dividing the spoil. The man's screams continued, the lions tore his limbs and started on his torso. Suddenly, there was silence. The lion who had clamped onto his neck had severed his head from his body. The silence was replaced by the sound of crunching bones and low growls. I felt nauseous.

I couldn't hear my companions scream. My eyes fixed on the spot where the man had been. The cheap air conditioning, Freon and ozone, floated with the man's image. My eyes drifted to blood and hair, part of the man's scalp stuck to the top of the window frame; it looked bent, probably from the force his shoulders had met in the small opening. He was still standing there, stinking, demeaning, teasing the lions. The preprogramed dialogue continued to play, but no one could hear it. Everyone was screaming again. They had never stopped.

One of the lions, possibly thinking there was more food on the other side of the bus's window, jumped up from the feast, its bloody paws entering the bus and holding to the window. It tried to pull itself in through the tight space, its head too big to fit. People screamed louder, they couldn't get further away. They crawled over one another thinking the back of the bus was safe. The courage and bravery of an ancient civilization inclined into mob rules and more screaming. My translator looked at me, her eyes still unbelieving. She spoke something in Chinese, the panic turning off the part of her brain that told her I wouldn't understand.

After several tries at trying to get an answer from me, she must have realized she wasn't speaking English.

"What are we going to do?"

"Wait for the tour to continue? Maybe we should throw the rest of the chickens out to the lions. It would at least keep them off of the bus."

She looked at me as if I was crazy. Maybe I was. I had a feeling that if the lions had been smart enough to distract the man and pull him out of the bus, they might be smart enough to get through a window or even open the front door.

"Tell them I'm coming through."

Li Ming yelled my instructions in Chinese. It took her several times, but finally the crowd parted. The lion that had been in the window had given up for the time being. I made my way to the chicken cage, grabbed a couple of volunteers, and threw them out the window. The lions immediately chased the chickens. In a few minutes, I had emptied the cage. I felt bad for the chickens.

The bus driver's head whirled around and spoke again. I looked at Li Ming, who had followed me.

"He asked everyone to sit down. The tour is about to continue."

I moved to the open window and tried to shut it. What was left of the man stared back at me, blood dripping down a few strands of hair. I looked past it, out the window, into the clearing. There wasn't anything recognizable left of the man on the ground, only some tattered and well-chewed clothing. Most of the lions were busy with what remained of the chickens. One was lying on its stomach, its tongue hanging out to one side, blood on its mouth and whiskers. It stared at me, licked its maw, and then seemed to smile. I laughed.

The window wouldn't close. The bus started to move. I returned to my seat. The driver spoke again. Li Ming translated.

"Thank you for taking the African Safari. We appreciate your business. You will be able to purchase souvenirs of your adventure at the gift shop."

Li Ming's voice was mechanical. She had returned to her job, the familiar, an escape from what she had just witnessed. I looked around me. The people had orderly returned to their seats, calmly, quietly. Did they believe that this had been part of the adventure?

I closed my eyes. The lion was still looking at me. I could smell the blood, feel the beast's heartbeat, and I knew why it had smiled at me. I had an ending.

Tastes like chicken.

PROJECT X-MAS

"Tourists."

"Tourists?"

It was more a statement of unbelief than a question.

"This isn't the first."

"You mean there have been others?"

The older man's look withered his subordinate. He didn't answer. York heard a familiar laugh.

"Sure, Lieutenant, lots more."

The sergeant who had been managing the clean-up bothered York. It wasn't his demeaning tone, or his appearance. At first, York thought it was a smell, or an irritating habit, but he could not find one specific thing about the man. The sergeant reminded him of bad food in a refrigerator, food that had gone from edible to unidentifiable. Like Goldstein, it was safely contained in a box behind the fridge door, but one day...

"You've read the files, haven't you?" asked Colonel Blackwell.

"Yes, sir."

York had read the files, re-read them several times, but seeing proof was different, strange; York wasn't sure what he believed anymore.

"These represent the few who didn't know how to drive," said Sergeant Goldstein. "Like Roswell."

There was a sneer on the man's face, as if he had made a joke that only he and the colonel thought was funny. York saw himself opening a forgotten container and the shock of seeing something growing inside. Goldstein looked at York like he was an outsider, or an intruder.

"How's it going, Joe?"

"Just about done, Colonel, the bodies are in the truck and what's left of the ship. The men are doing a final sweep to see if we missed anything."

"Good. The sooner we get out of here the better."

"What about the farmer, sir?" asked Goldstein.

"Lieutenant York and I were just going to talk to him."

The sergeant nodded; the smile on his face made York uncomfortable.

"That will be all, Joe."

"Yes sir."

The sergeant saluted, the colonel returned a tired attempt at military bearing.

"Let's go, York."

"Sir, no disrespect, but I thought—"

"Thought what, York? That flying saucers and aliens were science fiction?"

Blackwell's reaction was unexpected.

"Did you think you were being trained for some kind of exercise, that everything in the files was just a made up scenario?"

The colonel had stopped dead in his tracks, his eyes burned and York felt his skin crawl, trying to escape.

"No, nothing like that, I've read the flies, it's just that..."

"Just that what, York?"

The colonel aged when he was angry. York had only seen him from a distance, the old man they called him behind his back, but it had nothing to do with age. Colonel Blackwell had been there and done that more times than anyone.

"I just haven't read anything about survivors."

"Survivors?"

The colonel smiled and then laughed.

"You mean you thought this was just a research assignment, you'd be picking up pieces of evidence if you were lucky, and that you would never actually get your hands dirty?"

"Yes... Sir."

The colonel laughed again and started in the direction of the farmer, the witness. York followed. The last six months went through his mind.

York had graduated at the top of his class at the Naval Academy and had a promising career as a naval aviator ahead of him. He had never expected to be flying a desk, or to be recruited for a special mission.

He was told he had been hand selected by the President, although he wasn't sure now which president. He went through an intensive clearance process, then training in aircraft recognition, aerodynamics, and cutting edge technology. His background was in engineering, which was an obvious career for an aviator. There had been four of them at first, a friend from Annapolis and two from West Point. Soon, he was the only one left, and then he had been given a stack of files to read: Project X.

Project X was an unconfirmed project carried out by an unidentified agency in a non-existent branch of the government. It was an obvious and stupid name. Something no one would call a real project. The files contained reports, photos, and eye-witness accounts of unidentified flying objects, crash sites of unidentifiable aircraft, and, to his surprise, aliens. He thought it was an elaborate joke, an exercise of some kind, but he couldn't imagine what kind of exercise outside of an H.G. Wells novel.

"We do the job we're ordered to do, Lieutenant. Deal with your personal beliefs and opinions later."

Blackwell brought him back to the present.

"Yes sir."

Colonel Blackwell had stopped again. He stared at York for a long time. York felt like the older man was going to reveal something, something that would make sense of everything, or at least tell him they would talk later.

"Never mind," said the Colonel. "Just watch, observe, and don't say anything."

"Yes sir."

York followed Blackwell out of the containment area. There was a make-shift parking lot just over a small knoll that looked down into the crash site. Some local farmer, a ranch hand, had reported the crash. He was waiting when York and his team had arrived. How much he had seen, or knew, was yet to be determined. Blackwell arrived within seconds of the site being roped off.

"Hello, my name is Major Gunn, and this is my colleague, Lieutenant Daniels. I understand you reported the crash and saw what happened."

A private appeared and handed Blackwell a stack of cards. The colonel looked down, scanned them, and then returned to the witness.

"Mr. Pulsipher."

"Yeah, that's me, and I saw the flying saucer and the Martians that came in it."

"Flying saucer you say. How do you know they're Martians?" asked Blackwell.

York's mouth fell open. The response seemed to have the same effect on Pulsipher.

"You mean they really are aliens? Things from another planet? Like at Roswell?" asked Pulsipher.

"I don't know about that, Mr. Pulsipher. To the untrained eye, they might look like Martians, but from what I've heard on the radio and read in books, Martians are usually green, aren't they?"

"Yeah, that's true, but–"

"You can't really tell on these new televisions shows, everything's in black and white," interrupted Blackwell.

Pulsipher seemed to reconsider his answer. York could see the thought process and the outcome. What would his neighbors and co-workers think of his Martian story? Blackwell continued.

"These might be from Venus, or even as far away as Jupiter or Pluto. Did you see their ship before it crashed?"

York wanted to say something, but stopped himself. A subtle change was coming over Pulsipher.

"No, not really, I just saw the crash and drove out to see what happened."

"That's too bad," said Blackwell. "A flying saucer would have been a pretty good story, but at least you saw the aliens."

Pulsipher seemed to reconsider everything. He hadn't expected anyone to believe him. He looked at York and then back at Blackwell.

"Your just foolin' with me, aren't you, Major? Martians, aliens from another planet, that's just crazy talk."

"It's a better story than what really happened," said Blackwell.

Pulsipher considered Blackwell's response.

"So, what are they then?"

"The government would prefer it if people thought this was just another flying saucer story or another alien cover-up," said Blackwell.

"Cover-up?"

Colonel Blackwell looked at the card again and then back at Pulsipher.

"You go by Henry or Hank?"

"Hank."

"You mind if I call you Hank?"

"Not at all."

"Well, you see, Hank, I've got a real problem here. You've seen something that our government has been working on for several years, something that may end the Cold War and the Russian threat. Am I making sense?"

Pulsipher was a smart man, at least when it came to patriotism.

"A secret weapon."

"Something like that," said Blackwell.

"So, if I was to tell people I saw Martians and a flying saucer it would help the government keep it secret?"

"I guess it would, Hank. I've never thought about it that way."

"So, what is it really? Some kind of genetic program to engineer bodies that can survive traveling at the speed of light?"

Hank had quite an imagination. York smiled. The man obviously read a lot of science fiction.

"Hank, you know I'd really like to tell you, but…"

Blackwell paused for effect.

"I can see you're a smart man, someone I could trust, it's just that…"

Another pause. Hank nodded. York was watching a master at work. Blackwell got closer to Hank, almost as if he was going to tell him a real secret. He whispered his next words.

"You don't know how close to the truth you really are, Hank, but I can't confirm or deny any of this. I have my orders."

Blackwell winked at Hank. Hank smiled, as if he had just been let in on the biggest secret of the century. Blackwell backed up and continued.

"I hope we can trust you, Hank. Wouldn't want to have to come back this way and take you into custody or anything. You know what I mean."

"I was just thinking. I missed dinner. Think I might just mosey on back home."

"I think we'll be doing the same."

The farmer walked back to his pick-up truck. Blackwell waved to the headlights and watched Hank Pulsipher's taillights disappear in the dusty darkness of evening.

"You know he's going to tell everyone he sees about this," said York.

"By the time it makes it to the newspapers it will be a better story than any of us could have made up."

"But they'll report aliens and flying saucers."

"Not a whole lot we can do about that. I'm sure Hank will consider his story very carefully."

"Colonel," Goldstein interrupted. "We're ready to head back to base."

"Move 'em out, Joe."

"Yes sir."

York got in the lead truck with the sergeant, Sergeant Joseph Goldstein. The enlisted man had obviously been doing this for some time. Blackwell trusted him.

"So, Joe…"

"Sergeant Goldstein. When you've earned my respect, you can call me Joe, Lieutenant."

"Uh…"

York was speechless. He was an officer, but Joe did have a point. He didn't know what to make of this man. Goldstein had already made him.

"It's your first, you're confused, you don't know what to think, and then Blackwell didn't deny anything, just planted doubt."

"Yeah."

York looked out the window of the truck. He could see Blackwell enter the helicopter that had brought him to the site.

"I just can't believe we couldn't do anything to save them."

"I wouldn't worry too much about that, L.T. Not a lot we could have done."

Goldstein was right. What did they know of alien medicine.

"So, how long you been doing this, Sergeant Goldstein?"

"Seven years."

York nodded and sat back into his seat. The truck bounced and shook over the sage brush and other debris they had come over making a temporary road to the crash site. He tried to make the files fit in his mind. He could understand why they might have crashed. There was always danger in flight, and space flight had to be even more hazardous. There were so many things that could go wrong. The question that bothered him was why. Why would they come to Earth?

"Can I ask you something, Sergeant?"

"Sure, sir."

"The colonel said they were tourists, and then you said they didn't know how to drive. What does that mean?"

"Think about it. These things, aliens, whatever you want to call them, can come all the way across the galaxy without incident and then they just crash in the middle of nowhere. Seems like they don't know how to drive very well."

York had to agree. He even chuckled.

"As to the tourist thing, you've read the files. You know what the theory is. The evidence kind of proves it."

"Yeah, but that seems crazy, it –"

"As crazy as what's in the back of this truck?" interrupted Joe.

York thought about it for a moment. It wasn't all that crazy. York smiled. The Bible, the Torah, almost all the holy books pointed to the same thing. Maybe there was some truth in all the myth.

"What do you believe?"

"Shit, my people supposedly killed the savior of the universe, right on this planet, right in Jerusalem. If a god exists, a god that rules the universe, wouldn't these aliens know about it?"

"I guess, but wouldn't they be just like us?"

"You mean go to church on holidays, think about God for a couple minutes a year?"

York didn't reply. He had to put this into perspective. Goldstein interrupted.

"These aliens, they treat it like one of the Seven Wonders of the World. They want to see the place where God was crucified. They want to see what kind of people could do such a thing. We're aliens to them, barbarous aliens that would kill the being that created us."

York nodded again. They drove in silence for several miles. When the truck had made it onto a slightly improved road, Goldstein spoke again.

"I guess it's as plausible as anything else. I mean look at most Christians. They all want to see Jerusalem, Calvary, and the Sea of Galilee. The Moslems aren't much different. They dream of making the Haj, the trip to Mecca. If what the Torah says is true, God made the whole universe and everything in it, not just one planet with us on it. Why would aliens be that much different than us?"

"I guess there is only one Messiah," said York. "I never thought about it like that. It just seems funny, aliens making a pilgrimage to Earth."

"You do this job for a few years, L.T., and you'll be thinking about a lot of things differently.

York remained silent. Goldstein drove. It was several miles before he spoke again.

"What gets me is if all these aliens can travel across the stars, if they are so smart, why haven't they invented a time machine? They could go back and stop the whole thing if they wanted to, even take Jesus F. Christ back to their own planet."

"Or watch the event in real time," said York.

"Yeah, wouldn't that be something," said Goldstein.

York let the words float in and out of his head. He had never been a regular church goer, but he had read parts of the Bible. Goldstein had a valid point. It was as valid as flying saucers and aliens. He thought about aliens visiting Jerusalem.

"Do you think Christ would have gone with them?" asked York.

Joseph Goldstein didn't respond. They left the dirt road for asphalt. An hour passed, the lights of an airfield came into view.

"I guess they can't interfere. They have to let things play out," said York.

"If you believe the whole God, Jesus Christ, Creator of the Universe bull shit," said Goldstein.

"Or H.G. Wells," said York.

Sergeant Goldstein looked away from the road directly at York. A smile appeared on his lips and he laughed. He looked back to the road and continued driving.

"You read much, L.T.?"

"Yeah."

"What?"

"The classics, history, the newspaper."

"You ever read Jules Verne, Mary Shelley, Lovecraft?"

"Journey to the Center of the Earth, Twenty Thousand Leagues Under the Sea, Frankenstein…"

York's face changed, nostalgia seemed to be clouding his eyes, and then he smiled.

"I loved those stories."

Goldstein laughed, but it was a knowing laugh. York felt as if he had passed through a gateway, found a marker on a trail after being lost. The stories he loved as a child, a young man, stories he still loved played across his mind's eye.

It wasn't long until they had entered the base and approached the tarmac. An aircraft waited to be loaded and to take them back to where they had come from. As they were unloading the truck, the evidence, Goldstein spoke.

"I guess you're okay, L.T. You can call me Joe."

LOVECRAFT'S PILLOW

It floated like an indifferent storm cloud, hovering between the electric guitars and guns, undecided on its color or contents. A weathered 3 x 5 card slumped in front like a wounded aircraft in a boneyard. In another life, the card had been a coaster, the rings from sweating glasses or beer bottles merged with the black ink making the card's message hard to read.

The cotton slip peaked over the top of the card holding it in place; matching rings in varying shades of brown blended with the yellowish cast on the pillow case. The cotton count probably matched the pillow's age. The fabric had mellowed, the jaundice giving way to indistinct grays and browns. The colors cascaded through the store front window, into the cool air, and into my lungs making it hard to breathe. I shook my head, disbelieving. I read the card again, and then read it a third time aloud.

"Lovecraft's Pillow, Serious Inquiries Only."

There was a ghostly halo in the upper left-hand corner of the pillow; shapes of drool or a nighttime sneeze joined the occasional dark brown dot of blood from a nose or ear. I imagined the musty mold in the feathers, and my nose quivered; I took a deep breath, trying to clear my lungs and my imagination, and turned to resume my walk.

"Hey, watch where you're going."

My feet tripped over something dark and soft that moved with the sound of its voice. I maintained my balance and recognized the black impediment as a young woman: at least the hair and curves indicated as such.

"I'm so sorry," I said. "I didn't see you there."

"No harm done."

She stood, her eyes coming almost even with mine. Many months of trailers and ex-boyfriends smoldered in their depths. I blinked and took in her larger form.

Her flesh threatened to spill from the souvenir t-shirt she wore. Modified, sleeves detached, a slash making an improvised neckline; the silk-screened event it advertised was over before she was born. The story of her life spun itself in my mind. I felt funny, a little guilty, nodded, and resumed my walk. Before I could take a second step she placed a hand on my arm.

"Looking at the pillow?"

"Yes," I stuttered. "Yes, a good joke for Providence."

"Maybe," she said. "Maybe not."

Our eyes met again. Lightning flashed between her pupils, a forest fire breathing in their darkness. Hungry rats seemed to run up and down my spine, looking for food, their small claws and greasy tails against my skin. I blinked again. The girl was gone; a slice of time missing from my memory. My eyes reflected a mirage, and then I only saw my reflection in the glass of the pawn shop door. How had I moved without remembering? I thought about the pillow.

An odd feeling crept over my shoulders and down to my chest, that feeling just before the flu hits, empty and draining. I tried logic, but my position, standing at the entrance of the pawn shop, and the time that had passed between stumbling over the girl and moving to the doorway, was a mystery like a minor organ harvested without my knowledge.

I cleared the thought from my mind. Too many hours staring at a computer monitor looking for the right word or phrase, too much time spent in the cramped closet of storytelling: my profession had muddled my mind, or the dense air on the street, both in league, affecting my sense of place and time.

The girl was strange, possibly a hallucination, but finding myself at the entrance to the pawn shop was real. I looked back at the store front. The pillow was real. I couldn't rationalize a supernatural power, the air, or even the girl's strange aura as the culprits in my confusion. Maybe it was the pillow, Lovecraft's pillow.

I pulled open the door and entered. I would meet the creative entrepreneur with bad taste who put such an item on display.

It was what I expected, everything but the quiet aroma. A thin layer of dust perceptible at the very back of my throat mingled with the damp smell of body fluids. The racks and shelves ebbed with the flotsam and jetsam of people down on their luck, unemployed, or supporting a habit. Their stories waited to be claimed, most only half written before they were pawned, the protagonist intending on retrieving whatever he or she had left behind. The amount of merchandise whispered eternal writer's block waiting to write postmortem biographies.

I walked deeper into the depressing and oppressive den, the smell aging in a time machine of broken lives, changing to a mixture of used merchandise mingled with fear and unwanted sex. I anticipated the valuable stuff would be at the back, the brand name guitars and electronics, the hand guns and jewelry, under glass in a case that needed wiping. I wasn't disappointed. I was surprised there was no proprietor present. I expected an overweight, oily middle-aged man to apparate before my eyes.

I stepped to the counter and a tall, slightly stooped boy whose countenance reflected breeding gone awry approached from a dark corner. I must have missed him, like the girl, or the time walking from the storefront to the door. I imagined a hidden gargoyle standing sentinel over the refuse of lives lived badly. His eyes flickered, not cold, almost dead, matching his alabaster skin. I expected a connection between his brain and tongue would require voice activation on my part. I waited, gazing at the wares, not ready to speak, and thinking this lone ghoul would disappear like the girl.

"Get your pants on and come out here, I need dis place swept up."

The voice of a man was followed by the man himself, the man I had expected, but not the accent. I couldn't place it. He emerged from a beaded curtain, a mix of Marlon Brando and Southeast Asian jungle colliding with Cajun hoodoo. The wooden pieces of the curtain sounded dull as they brushed against each other, the air swallowing most of the sound before it reached my ears. The man saw me.

"We got us a customer, boy."

"I know," said the boy, unaccented.

The man wore a bullet-proof, polyester suit, the kind that takes on a shine with age. Sweat beaded across his forehead like snake oil and the movements of his hands betrayed cruelty, maybe perversion. He stopped to check his zipper, which he couldn't see, the image conjuring a sweat-stained scenario that had just taken place behind the beaded barrier. I was curious to see who was putting on their pants.

"Are ya gonna assist him?"

"He was looking around," said the boy.

The man's eyes seemed to function independent of each another and re-enforced my impression of the boy's pedigree. The man focused on him and me at the same time.

"Ya good for nothin' son of a… Excuse me, sir, I'm sorry. Cus-ta-ma' service is somethin' Jee-nee-us is still tryin' to master, ain't that right, Wilbur?"

The sarcasm was sharp, but did little damage. The boy had a fine-tuned sense of selective listening. His name raised a specter of E.B. White trapped in Orwell's *Animal Farm*.

"Ya jus' can' get good help deese days, even from your own kin."

He glared at the boy, which had as much effect as his venomous sarcasm. An inbred vibe permeated the conversation and raised a scent I had blocked: coitus interruptus. I thought of the pants again and didn't want to know who or what was putting them on. I felt ill, the imaginary flu returning.

I saw Lovecraft's elongated face in the boy and the man. The shop closed in, the air evaporated around me, and the residual perfume formed into juices digesting me slowly in the shop's stomach.

"Are a ya lookin' for somethin' in-pa-tick-yu-la?"

The man was approaching fast, an uncoiling serpent, grease ebbing from the large pores and pock marks that were growing in size the nearer he came. I feared he would extend a hand in greeting and I would be obligated to shake it, a thick, tepid liquid turning to napalm on my skin.

"I'm John Whateley."

Whateley? Where had I heard that name?

"What can I help ya find?"

My mind went blank: the girl, the boy, the man, all more frightening than nightmares, more unbelievable than the fiction I wrote. I cleared my throat, focused, and tried to make sense of the weird voice speaking a warning in my inner ear.

"I noticed the pillow in the window."

"Ah, da pillow."

The uncoiling movement forward stopped giving Whateley the appearance of retreat. The look of an easy sale turned to something akin to apprehension. I couldn't understand it. Why would Whateley be afraid of making a sale, of conning a stranger into buying a gag pillow?

"Did ya read da card?" asked Whateley.

"Serious inquiries only," I said.

Whateley nodded, his eyes turning gibbous, an impish smile brewing beneath his downturned lips. He turned to speak to the boy.

"Wilbur, go an' see what's takin' Lavinia so long."

Wilber, Lavinia, Whateley, names I was certain came from a tale of inbreeding and horror, a tale that would match the pillow, a Lovecraft tale. My mind cleared, I remembered the story, and smiled: Whateley was overdoing his act just to sell a pillow.

"So, ya in-tear-ested in Lovecraft?" asked Whateley. "You're problee a writer or somethin'. Ya want ta know if dat pillow is gen-yu-wine."

"Something like that," I said.

"If you're interested in Lovecraft, ya problee noticed da names too, problee thinkin' me and ma kin are an act for city folk, a spec-tee-cal to draw in un-soo-speck-tin rubes off da street."

I agreed with Whateley. "The names seem to cheapen the charade," I said, "or should I say add charm to your shop."

Whateley chuckled. I thought of a caged wolverine poked one too many times with a sharp stick.

"Dat's why da sign says seer-ee-us in-queer-ees only."

I nodded again, waiting for Whateley to continue.

"Well, Mista, Mista… I don bee-leeve I got your name."

"You didn't, but my inquiry is serious, not so much about the pillow, but where you got the idea, Mr. Whateley, if that's your real name."

Whateley chuckled again.

"It is."

Whateley's eyes changed to a reflection of mirth, but only on the surface; in their depths I sensed something sinister, a reminder of something darker, something buried in old books, or beneath the sea, waiting to be loosed on an unsuspecting public. I was the wedding guest, held fast by the gaze of the Ancient Mariner. The discordant timber of the beaded doorway broke the spell.

"Where do you want me to start, Pa?

The girl I had nearly stumbled over emerged, the same sensation of damaged goods emanating from what little of her personality I had experienced. Images of Whateley and whatever happened behind the bamboo curtain brought bile to the back of my throat. There couldn't have been enough time for such a depraved act, but time was not making sense anymore. In this world, Whateley's world, anything was possible. Whateley's disheveled appearance told its own story.

"Hello again," the girl said.

Whateley looked at me and then back at his daughter.

"Ya know dis man?"

"We've crossed paths," said Lavinia, a waggish gleam in her eyes. "He's interested in the pillow."

It was becoming obvious Lavinia was mature beyond her years and probably needed an antibiotic infused bath and a lesson in dental hygiene. Whateley seemed confused, either by the unlikely acquaintance of his daughter with me, or a secret knowledge of something that was too senseless not to be true. I had been baited, hooked, and reeled in. Whateley cleared his throat.

"Jus' finish sweepin' up and den mop da floor."

Something was wrong. Whateley's tone had shifted. The two children's language was too normal. The demeaning sarcasm he unleashed on the boy had turned to an almost kind trepidation in speaking to the girl. I stood still as his attention returned to me.

"Dair mudda was quite da reeda'," said Whateley. "She loved Lovecraft, married me for ma name. I had nothin' ta do with namin' da kids, but jus' like in da story, da Missus up and dies on me, leaves me with two young'uns an' dat damned pillow."

I nodded without empathy. Whateley turned back to his daughter.

"If someone comes in, I'll be in ma office."

Lavinia nodded, turned, and our eyes met again. I felt naked, her gaze weighing and measuring me as if I was property to be pawned. This young harpy could eat me up and spit me out. Even the rats running up and down my spine shivered.

"Let's go back ta ma office and chat, Mista...?"

"King," I lied.

We walked through the bamboo beaded doorway into a dimly lit room that looked and smelled like the warren of a hoarder in a hot house.

"So, you're wonderin' if it's ree-al," said Whateley.

"Yes," I said.

That was the question, and the sooner I had the answer, the sooner I could leave. Whateley directed me to an office. There were two chairs and a couch. I chose a chair for sanitary reasons, imagined and real. The aged fluorescent light cast a shade like the aged pillow case on the room.

Whateley reclined on the couch, its contours familiar to his bulbous girth, which had been partially hidden until he sat down. I was regretting entering this incestuous shop, meeting Whateley and his progeny, and sitting down.

"Have a drink."

Whateley opened an ice chest next to the couch, found a can, and tossed it to me before I could decline. The PBR only added to the reality. I was sure this was not a dream.

"I can't prove nuthin' 'bout da pillow. I can only tell ya what I know."

I opened the Pabst and feigned a sip. Whateley drained a can in a single swallow, reached for another, opened it, and drained about half. I expected a belch to mingle with the coitus stained couch.

"Ma wife acquired da pillow when she was in Arkham several years ago. Said she found it at a gee-rage sale. If ya ask me, dat damn pillow is what killed her."

"What do you mean?" I asked, interested enough to hear a little more of Whateley's scam.

"I loved dat woman."

Whateley finished his second beer and opened a third. His face took on the sheen of someone who has difficulty moving his bowels. I wasn't sure if it was the loss of his wife or too much beer too quickly that brought the verdant change to his face. A little adjusting on the couch and his normal bleached countenance returned. The beer seemed to improve his diction as well.

"She insisted on sleepin' on it, and dat's when da dreams began."

I nodded, not believing a single word of the fat man's story.

"She would wake up an' tell me things, things she saw, dark and evil things. Other times, she'd tell me da future, 'bout a customer, an ax-cee-dent goin' to happen, and dey all came true. She even predicted Wilbur and Lavinia's births, da day, da hour, and da minute. I tried to get rid of da cursed thing, but she wouldn't' have it. When Lavinia was 'bout five-years-old, she took a likin' to dat pillow. I come home from work one day and found Lavinia next to ma wife, holdin' the pillow tight. My wife had a gun in 'er 'and, and dare was a pool of..."

Whateley trailed off. I could imagine the scene and what would come next, but it didn't come. Whateley sniffed.

"Nuthin' good ever come from dat pillow."

I nodded, only wanting to leave. I set the beer down on the floor.

"I tried to get rid a da thing, but it kept comin' back. I thought Lavinia was gettin' it outta da trash. I tore it up in a million pieces, but it didn' matte' none."

"What do you mean?" I asked.

"It put itself back togetha', like it had nevuh been torn up."

Whateley paused again.

"I tried burnin' it, sendin' it out with da trash, but it wouldn't leave. Lavinia seemed too connected to da thing, so I put it up for sale, hopin' someone would take it away and keep it."

I was almost starting to believe Whateley.

"Sold it once, real cheap, five bucks; thought dat was da end of it."

"What happened?" I asked.

"Showed up in a lot I bought at an ee-state sale up Boston way. Had no idea it was part a da purchase 'til I went through da stuff. I recognized it like it was ma own face. Come ta find out later da previous owner was who I'd sold it to. Da owner had a seer-ee-us ack-see-dent."

I smiled and got up to leave. I had heard enough.

"So, ya interested in buyin' it?"

"No, I don't think so," I said.

"I'll make ya a good price. In fact, ya can take it, try it out for a week or two, and den pay me what you think it's worth."

I wasn't sure what Whateley meant by trying it out for a week or two. The obvious meaning was too degenerate to consider and too disgusting. Who would sleep with the filth of the Whateley family, especially with whatever had seeped into the thing from his wife's—

"No, I think I'll pass on this one," I said.

"How 'bout if I give it to ya? You can have it," said Whateley.

Everything I had thought about the man changed. His cheap carny trickery had vanished replaced by something I couldn't recognize. I looked at him. Deep, in the backs of his eyes, there was something cold, something damp. My heart stopped and started. It was fear.

"I need to be on my way."

"Please, Mista King, jus' take it. I don' wan' it in ma store."

"I don't believe anything you've told me," I said.

"Fine, dat's fine, Mista King, jus' take it with ya, throw it in da garbage on your way home, or wherever you're goin'. "Pleese, Mista King, jus' take it. I don' wan' it in ma store," said Whateley. "I would be much obliged."

If this was salesmanship, it was the kind akin to Br'er Rabbit and the Briar Patch. For a moment, I wavered.

""How much?"

"What?" asked Whateley.

"How much for the pillow?" I asked again.

I knew there would be a price after all this bad acting, but Whateley seemed to lose all sense of thought, let alone any dickering skill. This was the weirdest fraud I had ever seen. I had entered a nightmare world and would wake up, blink my eyes, and Whateley, his children, and the pillow would all be gone. Whateley moved to the edge of the couch.

"Ya seer-ee-us?"

"Dead serious," I said.

The sound of blunted wood beads, the scent of Lysol and lubricant, and then the shadow of Lavinia appeared in the office doorway.

"I'm done, Pa. What do you need me to do next?"

Up close, I made an effort not to look at her. I wanted to imagine her repulsive in a wanton kind of way, but that only made her striking. She looked at me, I could feel her eyes, and when I met them her father's lurking grin stared back at me behind her downturned lips. The smells of unhallowed acts washed over me and I stepped to the side, knocking over my unfinished beer.

"Oh, I'm sorry."

"Let me get that," said Lavinia.

The girl moved like an experienced pole dancer; her words, her actions, all displayed a raw desire for the forbidden, a teasing helpfulness pouring out of her into the room. I could understand Whateley now, his wife and children, and I almost believed his story.

"How much?" I asked again.

"For the pillow," said Lavinia.

It wasn't a question and I felt the blood rise in my cheeks. I coughed.

"Yes, for the pillow."

"You aren't selling the pillow again, are you, Pa?"

Whateley tried to quiet his daughter without being obvious. He failed.

"Have you sold it before?" I asked.

"I already told ya 'bout it," said Whateley.

Something wasn't right.

"How many times have you sold it?" I asked.

Whateley looked at his daughter. If looks could kill, Lavinia was impervious to Death. Her father's anger only made her more belligerent.

"He only told you about the estate sale, didn't he?"

I nodded.

"Ask him about the others, the ones that owned it before my ma."

"Dat's jus' made up stuff," said Whateley. "What dat woman she bought it from told her."

"No it's not, it's all true," said Lavinia.

"How can you know dat," sneered Whateley.

"It told me."

Her words were as if Whateley's cooler had been dropped from a great height onto my head and the contents of cans and ice dumped on my prone body. I couldn't believe it. I looked around the room. A pallor had come over the fat man that was palpable. Lavinia looked at me, willing a shock collar around my neck. I was afraid to speak.

"The pillow knows the truth. Ma knew it, and so do I."

Whateley withered under his daughter's glare. I had the dynamics of this family all wrong, and the disagreement between how Whateley spoke to his children explained itself. Lavinia turned to face me. I tensed expecting a jolt, worse if I didn't respond.

"It's true enough. Howard got all his weird stories out of that pillow, and there's plenty more waiting. You just have to know how to keep the nightmares inside."

"Howard?" I cautioned. "Lovecraft?"

Lavinia had taken on an eerie glow as if she was turning into a crystal ball. Her father had surrendered, melting back into the couch.

"A page from the mad Arab's book, sand from a lost city, all stuffed in, and before that it lay on a bed in a city now sunken beneath the sea."

Lovecraft's stories were remembering themselves in my mind.

"Mary found the dreams inside."

"Mary?" I whispered.

"Yeah, Mary, Mary Shelby, Mary Shelvy, something like that, you know, the monster?"

"Mary Shelley? Frankenstein?" I asked.

"Yeah, that Mary."

For a brief second, sanity returned. Whateley's play was beginning act two. One look at the old man told me otherwise.

"You're a writer, aren't you?" asked Lavinia.

Her eyes burned black and images of bad school days and sodomy laws scratched my heart. Lavinia's lips inverted into a smile. My bladder winked like a caution light.

"I knew you were a writer when I saw you outside. Ma used to say the pillow had lots of stories still in it, it was a writer's pillow, said it was old, even older than Jesus Christ."

"Judas Iscariot," I whispered.

"I don't know," said Lavinia, "but Mary had it, then Po' Boy, and then Howard."

"Po' Boy?"

"Yeah, Ma, called him Po, her Po' Boy."

"Poe, you mean Edgar Allan Poe?"

"Maybe, I don't know."

The story was too convincing, too good to be true, and a moment of clarity freed my feet that had frozen in the pooling beer. I smiled and started for the beads and the exit. I was done with this made up family and their made up story, although I had to admit, it was a good story. The smells and sounds only added to its delivery.

"You leaving without hearing the rest?" said Lavinia. "You don't want to hear about Daphne du Maurier, or Shirley Jackson, or Sylvia Plath. I really liked Sylvia."

I stopped in my tracks and then found myself laughing.

"What's so funny" asked Lavinia.

"You can't remember Mary Shelley or Edgar Allan Poe's names, and suddenly you spit out three complete names?"

I continued to laugh. Lavinia remained stone-faced. I was done with this place and with these bumpkins. They were creative in a depraved squalor kind of way. I turned to face Whateley. The blood rushed from my face.

What had been an overweight, ignorant excuse for a circus barker had turned into a shivering mass of glutinous terror. The sheen of sweat that covered his face had blended with the shine of his suit and a dark stain had spread in his pants. His eyes pleaded, begging me to stop, or maybe take him with me. I was baffled. I had to force myself to look away, but only found Lavinia staring at me with fiery hourglass eyes, a black widow.

"I think I better leave."

Whatever had looked like an over-exuberant and unkempt girl with a penchant for sexual innuendo had become a dark and dangerous predator who did not like being laughed at.

"No," said Lavinia.

Her command activated more than my imagined shock collar. I froze.

"I remember them because they're still fresh like Howard."

"What?" I asked.

"Most of them only needed to sleep on it once, just needed to look into the abyss, see what was there, and then they could write. One nightmare was enough to keep them going."

"What are you talking about?" I asked.

"Sylvia kind of got attached to it. It didn't work out so well?"

I turned to leave, but Lavinia's voice brought me to a standstill.

"I think you better complete your transaction with my father."

I responded slowly and succinctly. "I don't want the pillow."

"You don't have a choice. The pillow wants you."

The revelation was a joke, but only on the surface. Lavinia stared at me with a force I could feel, and then turned Medusa on her father, who jumped off the couch and went to his desk. The pen in his hand, the receipt book, a blur; before I knew it, an invoice was in my pocket and Lavinia was leading me to the window display. This was not happening.

"Don't worry too much, Mr. King," Lavinia said. "You can bring it back after you've slept on it."

There was no way in hell I was going to sleep on that thing, let alone touch it. Lavinia read my mind.

"Pa, get a sack. The pillow is going to have to do some convincing."

I stood stunned to silence.

"It knows what you're thinking. Believe me; it isn't just going to let you walk away or dump it somewhere. It will wait for you. Take my advice, you sleep on it, get it over with, and then you can bring it back."

Lavinia paused. The hidden grin was breaking on her lips and I found myself staring at her womanhood. An unbidden desire ascended from the depths of my soul, an act that sickened me, but felt inevitable. Lavinia's eyes seemed to undress and violate me as a passing thought, and then pearly white teeth appeared leering at me.

"You can bring it back…"

Lavinia paused, the smile still glowing.

"…if you can walk."

ABOUT THE AUTHOR

K. Scott Forman is a writer and editor. He co-edited and contributed to the first three volumes of *Fast Forward: A Collection of Flash Fiction* along with working on three more volumes, a novel, and a flash novel for Fast Forward Press. He also edited *It Came from the Great Salt Lake: A Collection of Utah Horror* and has published several short stories and poems. He was the recipient of the Robert Creeley Scholarship in 2007 at Naropa University, and graduated with a Master of Fine Arts degree in 2009. Scott teaches English Composition at Weber State University, and was an adjunct faculty member at the National Cryptologic School. He is a member of the Horror Writers Association (HWA) and enjoys long walks in inclement weather, sunsets with blood in them, and Metallica at volumes determined unsafe by the Surgeon General. He currently is at work on the Great American Novel. He makes his home in the Rocky Mountains with his family and a collection of guitars.